EGMONT

We bring stories to life

First published in Great Britain in 2020
by Egmont Books UK Limited
2 Minster Court, London EC3R 7BB

Text copyright © 2020 Annabelle Sami
Illustrations © 2020 Allen Fatimaharan

The moral rights of the author and illustrator have been asserted

ISBN 978 1 4052 9699 1

A CIP catalogue record for this title is available from the British Library

70802/001

Printed and bound in Great Britain by CPI Group

Stay safe online. Any website addresses listed in this book are
correct at the time of going to print. However, Egmont is not
responsible for content hosted by third parties. Please be aware
that online content can be subject to change and websites can
contain content that is unsuitable for children. We advise that
all children are supervised when using the internet.

MIX
Paper from
responsible sources
FSC® C020471

LLAMA OUT LOUD

OUT LOUD

ILLUSTRATED BY
ALLEN FATIMAHARAN

ANNABELLE SAMI

EGMONT

To my very own loud and loving family:
Mum, Dad and Chloe. This book would
not exist without you. Love you.

CHAPTER ONE
Unbelieeeeeevable!

There are some stories that are hard to believe. If you're smart (which I can already tell you are, dear reader) then you won't believe everything you're told. For instance, I've never trusted fairy tales. I mean, come on. Do they expect us to believe that you can survive being eaten by a wolf? I'm also pretty sure that a house made of gingerbread would melt in the rain, or at least attract a few flies.

Since you're clever, I'm sure you've always questioned those horror stories about kids that lost all their teeth eating too many sweets. Maybe you've watched a film and annoyed your friends by saying, 'That would never happen in real life!'

Well, I'll be honest with you. This story *is* hard to believe. But unlike a fairy tale, it doesn't take place in a faraway kingdom. Instead, we'll be travelling to the streets of Whitechapel in East London – a place you might hear the locals call 'The Ends' – where you can buy a samosa for a pound or a rainbow-coloured bagel from the many street vendors on Brick Lane. People from all around the world live under this one postcode, and even more come to visit on Sundays when the market is in full swing. It's a small corner of London, but there's a *whole world* inside it. And, despite what you might be thinking, the hero of our story isn't some cockney geezer. It's a girl – Yasmin.

Oh, and a llama. A toy one, of course, not a real one. That would be weird.

By now you must be thinking, that *does* sound unbelievable!

I know. But believe me. It's *real*.

P.S. There's one more thing you should know about Yasmin. You see, her parents haven't stopped talking since 1991 and her brothers might as well be

in training for the Most Annoying event at the Olympics. Not to mention Yasmin's aunties, who always think they know best. Of course, Yasmin still loves them, but all the hubbub results in Yasmin making a very particular choice. A choice she upholds even to this day . . .

Actually – I can't be bothered to do a flashback yet. Let's just get to the story, hey? I'm sure you'll find out what you need to know soon enough.

So where were we . . .? Oh yes. (Cue dramatic music.)

Life as Yasmin had known it, for a whole nine years and 363 days, was about to change.

Forever.

CHAPTER TWO
Bargain Hunt

Yasmin was staring at the ugliest toy llama she had ever seen. It was in the £2.99 bargain bucket in Old Spitalfields market, with one dodgy eye that bulged out and wonky ears. A few tattered pieces of cloth hung around its neck as decoration. The stains all over its back legs were a worrying brown colour. Even £2.99 seemed way too expensive to Yasmin. You would have to pay HER to take the thing home.

And yet she couldn't stop staring at it. It was one of those situations where something is just so disgusting that you *have* to look – like a squished snail on the garden path (and Yasmin had been guilty of quite a few snail casualties). The llama held her with its beady little glass eyes and it was starting to give her the creeps.

Yasmin didn't usually come to the market after school. It was a crowded, covered square filled with everything you could ever need, from tablecloths to teapots. Yasmin often thought it was worrying that most of her clothes were bought from the same stall that sold toilet brushes. Walking around, it was easy to get confused in the maze of tables and the noisy, bellowing yells of the vendors. Today, just like any other busy afternoon, it was teaming with people who swarmed like ants around the colourful

6

stalls. Actual ants also swarmed around the back of the food tents, trying to find falling crumbs to feast on.

It was noisy, smelly and definitely *not* the place that Yasmin would have chosen to spend the afternoon. But as usual, she had no choice. Even though it was her tenth birthday.

As the chosen School Representative, Yasmin had just made her weekly visit to the local elderly daycentre as part of a community programme.

(More on that later.) But instead of taking her home, Auntie Bibi had cheerily grabbed her hand and yanked her in the direction of the market.

'I thought we might do some shopping, Yassy! What do you think?' she chirped. 'I knew you'd be pleased. You love shopping, just like your auntie!'

Yasmin sighed and patted her auntie's hand. She actually hated shopping. But if it would make her auntie happy, then she would grin and bear it. Yasmin was good at keeping other people happy.

As soon as they were through the gates, Auntie Bibi made a beeline for a stall selling an array of brightly coloured scarves.

'There's the one I saw earlier!' she chimed. 'Isn't it beautiful?'

Yasmin thought the scarf looked like a giant feather duster.

'You're right. I *should* get more than one,' Auntie Bibi agreed, as if Yasmin had suggested it. Yasmin always marvelled at her auntie's ability to hold a

8

conversation entirely by herself.

Deciding to make the best of things, Yasmin pointed to the small arts-and-crafts stall nestled in the centre of the market. There was a big wooden box filled with high-quality colouring pencils for sale, the kind Yasmin dreamed of owning for her sketches.

Her auntie pushed her hand aside. 'Who wants boring pencils when you could have a pretty scarf?' she said. 'Come now. Doesn't this look pretty?!'

Whilst her auntie tried on scarves for the fifty millionth time (she couldn't choose between the fluorescent yellow or the sicky green), Yasmin had wandered towards the arts-and-crafts stall – and come across the previously mentioned llama.

Against her better judgment, she reached out and picked it up. It was soft and surprisingly warm, which made Yasmin feel a bit sick.

The market trader rubbed his hands together, sensing a sale. 'You want it, sweetheart?'

Yasmin dropped the llama back in the box and sprayed her hands with the antibacterial gel she always carried. Her parents had told her not to talk to strangers. Especially ones selling low-end stuffed toys at unreasonable prices.

'Oh, how cute!' Auntie Bibi's voice came ringing over Yasmin's shoulder. 'It reminds me of a toy donkey I had when I was a little girl. Do you want it, Yassy?'

Yasmin shook her head vigorously. But Auntie Bibi had already taken out her purse and was handing the market trader two shiny pounds.

'Wonderful! You're going to have so much fun together.' She plopped the toy into Yasmin's schoolbag, already directing Yasmin towards the exit. 'Your Auntie Bibi always gets you the best presents. Now we need to get home. Dinner is almost ready.'

'It's £2.99, love,' the trader called after them.

'You're lucky I even gave you two pounds!' Auntie

Bibi smiled sweetly and continued walking away.

Yasmin blinked. Within the space of what felt like a few seconds, she had managed to become the owner of what looked like a failed science experiment that she definitely *did not want*.

And things were only going to get stranger.

CHAPTER THREE
No Ordinary (Birth)day

In terms of best days in the year, the order for most children goes:

Third place – last day of school

Second place – Christmas (or Eid for Yasmin)

First place – BIRTHDAY!!

But more often than not, what should have been the best day of the year for Yasmin was just like any other day. And, just like any other day, as Yasmin and Auntie Bibi turned the corner on to their road, they could hear yells coming from the Shah family home.

Number 11 Fish Lane was the last to be built on the road, and had been squished in between the furthest two houses on the street. This meant that the house was extremely tall and extremely thin, with one room on each floor. If it hadn't been

sandwiched between two other houses, it would probably have toppled over in a strong breeze.

Yasmin's room was all the way up in the attic, while the bathroom was in the basement. The strange layout of number 11 meant that Yasmin had to walk up through every family member's bedroom before she could get to her own. Being at the top of the house was good for privacy, but it also meant that you had to be careful after eating a spicy curry from Brick Lane. Yasmin was sure she could rival any Olympic sprinter running down those stairs in the middle of the night, desperate for the loo.

As Yasmin and Auntie Bibi came in through the kitchen door, they were hit by a wall of sound that Auntie Bibi immediately added to.

'We're home!!!' she sang, heading over to Ammi, who was sweating over a boiling pot of rice.

'WHYAREYOULATEDINNERISREADYGOGET CHANGED!'

Ammi only spoke in shouts and never expected

an answer, even if she asked a question.

'These potatoes need coriander! I always say add coriander!' Papa yelled at no one in particular.

'Papaaaaaa!' Tall Brother roared. 'Tariq *accidently* spilled curry paste on Yasmin's chair.'

Short Brother smirked. 'Whoops! Clumsy me . . .'

Yasmin scowled. That curry-paste spill was no accident. It would have to be soaked overnight in Ammi's special baking-soda concoction.

'I guess you'll have to sit on the wonky stool at the end of the table, Yasmin,' Tall Brother sniggered.

'I hope you didn't get any curry paste on my seat at the head of the table. A father should always sit at the head of the table,' Papa shouted, angrily stirring his potatoes.

Auntie Bibi giggled and patted her younger brother on the head. Papa hated it when she did that and immediately smoothed his hair down in the reflection of the fridge.

'Ammi, I'm laying the table but Tariq isn't helping!'

Tall Brother called out.

'Yes I am!' Short Brother bellowed.

'No you're not!'

Unnoticed, Yasmin hurried up the stairs, leaving the noise and the thick aromas of curry and daal behind. She needed a moment of peace away from her family before dinner.

On the floor above the kitchen was the room that Auntie Bibi shared with Auntie Gigi. The aunties were twins, and had lived with Yasmin ever since she was born. It would have been strange not to hear their thunderous snores every night, or their endless gossiping at all hours of the day.

As Yasmin passed through her aunties' room, the smell of perfume washed over her. She inhaled the sweet smell deeply before noticing her Auntie Gigi, who was applying incredibly thick eyeliner in the mirror. She looked like a panda who had melted in the oven. Why people made such a fuss over makeup, Yasmin would never know.

'Yassy darling, could you put my shoes on for me? You know I can't bend down nowadays, my back won't let me.'

Yasmin didn't want Auntie Gigi to snap in half, so she did as she was asked. With much pushing and tugging, the shoes went on. Auntie Gigi sighed in relief.

'Well done, flower. Now go and get your party dress on.' Auntie Gigi winked.

Both of Yasmin's aunties were shopping fanatics. However often Yasmin politely protested, Auntie Gigi would still buy flouncy, frilly outfits for her to wear – outfits that Yasmin would never choose herself. But because she knew her auntie was just trying to be nice, Yasmin bit her lip, forced a smile and took herself off up the next flight of stairs.

In her parents' bedroom, everything was in military-level order as usual. Ammi would accept nothing less. The same couldn't be said for her brothers' room on the floor above. They had left the

TV playing a particularly noisy and violent programme, and Short Brother's PE kit was in a stinking pile on the floor. (Yasmin usually referred to her siblings as 'Tall Brother' and 'Short Brother' as their heights were, quite honestly, the most interesting thing about them.)

Yasmin paused at their door with a grin. A year earlier, her brothers had hung up a sign that said 'No Girls Allowed' in big, red letters. They obviously hadn't thought it through, since Yasmin *had* to go through their room to get to hers. She liked to rub this in by grinning at the sign every time she swanned through.

As she entered her little attic bedroom and slung her schoolbag in the corner, Yasmin felt her shoulders relax for the first time. She had decorated her room to include all the things she liked. There was a big poster about the ancient Egyptians on her ceiling (Yasmin loved history) and she had painted the wall behind her bed like a chalkboard. It was filled with little doodles and ideas that popped into her head just before she went to sleep. She thought of drawing a special birthday doodle, but the inspiration left her when she saw the dress that Auntie Gigi had bought, laid out neatly on the bed and wrapped in a pink bow. It was lime green with embroidered jewels around the bottom and, of course, a pair of matching sparkly shoes.

Auntie Gigi had written a little note on the top.

Dear Yasmin
This colour will look beautiful against your long, shiny black hair (which you got from me by the way!)
Kisses xxxx

Yasmin rolled her eyes. What was wrong with a pair of jeans? Dresses just made her feel . . . icky.

Suddenly inspiration struck again. She knew exactly what she wanted to draw. With a little smirk, Yasmin picked up her black sketch book and began drawing one of her favourite doodles: a comic strip she called 'Secret Agent Yasmin' (or SAY for short). In each comic strip, she had a different mission. Flipping through to find a blank page, Yasmin saw some of her earlier masterpieces such as THWART TALL BROTHER'S PRANK. For her latest edition, the mission was clear: AVOID WEARING UGLY DRESS.

Yasmin examined her finished masterpiece. It hadn't lifted her spirits. All of the comics she drew were fun . . . but they were just *daydreams*. She never had the confidence to act on any of them.

Yasmin picked the dress up and tossed it into the corner of the room, wishing that a sinkhole would suddenly appear and slurp the dress away into the depths of the earth. She stomped over and blew a raspberry at the crumpled heap. It was no use trying to fight her family's wishes. She would have to wear it, or she'd be labelled rude and ungrateful.

Tonight, there would be no favourite smelly trainers and jeans.

Tonight, like every night, Yasmin would have to wear the clothes her aunties wanted her to wear.

And eat the food her parents wanted her to eat.

And sit where her brothers wanted her to sit.

Even though it was her tenth birthday.

CHAPTER FOUR
Feeding Time in
the Lion's Den

The kitchen was chaos. All six family members placed bowls of steaming food, chutneys and lemonade on the table whilst shouting about what should go where. Yasmin crept in, wearing her new dress. It was probably best just to sit quietly at the table, like she usually did. But unfortunately, Short Brother had already spotted her.

'So . . . did you win your checkers match this afternoon, Yasmin?' he asked, trying to act like he was too cool to care.

'Or have all the oldies turned into fossils?' Tall Brother smirked.

Yasmin pointed to the 'winner' badge she had pinned to her party dress and took a sip of lemonade. She had been competing in the checkers tournament at the elderly people's daycentre for a few weeks now and had won every match. It was a game that required concentration, logic and *quiet* – some of Yasmin's favourite things. The focused calm that surrounded a game of checkers made Yasmin feel like she was wrapped in a nice warm blanket. Even if she didn't win the tournament, she was *sure* she could make it to the finals.

'Phhhst.' Tall Brother rolled his eyes. 'You won't win the whole thing.'

'Yeah, no chance,' Short Brother added, quick to copy his brother.

Yasmin ignored them both and got up to help Papa and Ammi with the chapattis.

'How is school?' Papa asked as she passed him a handful of flour.

'DIDYOUPASSTHESPELLINGTEST?' Ammi added.

'Of course she did, she's great at spelling.'

'SHEGOTTHATFROMME.'

Yasmin gritted her teeth. This was her *birthday celebration*. Weren't birthdays meant to be fun? All her parents wanted to do was talk about school.

'For your science project I have decided we will study moss growth and reproduction,' Papa told Yasmin. 'That is what I studied at university, therefore I am very knowledgeable on the subject.'

'But how will moss growth help her grades?

I think she should study the water cycle,' Auntie Gigi called over from the table.

'Do not question me, sister. I am the man of the house.'

'Man of the house or not, you are still our younger brother!' Auntie Bibi countered.

'COMEONEVERYONEDINNERISREADY.' Ammi's voice cut through the hubbub. She was the one person nobody ever questioned.

'Yassy, are you coming to sit down?' Auntie Bibi asked.

Yasmin took a deep breath and walked over to the table with a sour face. She may have to sit through this meal, but she didn't have to smile.

'One more thing before we eat.' Papa seemed very pleased with himself as he produced a square parcel wrapped in red paper out of his briefcase. 'A present for Yasmin.'

Yasmin's eyes grew wide. Maybe her parents did care about her birthday after all! Carefully peeling

26

open the paper, she uncovered her birthday present.

Smiths Bumper Book of Logic and Reasoning Puzzles – proven to increase brain activity!

Yasmin stared at it in silence, trying to muster a grateful smile. Her brothers giggled.

'Yasmin will have the most active brain in her whole class.' Papa beamed. 'Now let's discuss your maths grades –'

Yasmin managed to get through the dinner without throwing her rubbish present through the window. Then, finally, it was time for dessert. And Ammi had made a birthday cake!

'Your Ammi spent all afternoon baking this cake, Yasmin,' Auntie Bibi prompted.

Yasmin's face softened and she smiled up at Ammi. The cake was double-tiered chocolate, with beautiful buttercream flowers on the top. The family collectively gasped at its absolute chocolatey amazingness.

Ammi carried the heavy cake to the table with such care that it might as well have been a newborn baby. She gently placed it in front of Yasmin and was *just* about to light the candles . . . when Yasmin opened her napkin.

Pepper puffed out of the napkin's folds.

It rose into Yasmin's nose in a big cloud of spiciness, causing a loud –

'ACCCHOOOO!'

Nobody moved.

Sounding like a plug popping out of the plughole, Yasmin unstuck her face from the icing.

For once, the whole family was quiet. Through icing-coated eyelashes, Yasmin could see that they were all staring at Ammi and holding their breath.

Ammi looked at Yasmin.

Yasmin looked at Ammi.

Auntie Gigi looked at her own napkin and then used it to wipe Yasmin's face.

Then, in the loudest voice ever to come out of Ammi's mouth – the equivalent of a jet engine *and* an earthquake – Yasmin's mother boomed:

'YASMIIIIIIIIIIIIIIIN!YOURUINEDTHECAKE!'

Yasmin's brothers cackled with laughter. Tall Brother slyly picked up the pepper shaker and wiggled it teasingly at Yasmin. Her parents always seemed to miss their pranks.

'Because of your outburst –' (Outburst? thought Yasmin. It was a *sneeze!*) '– Ammi's cake is ruined!

Why didn't you blow your nose before dinner?'
Papa ranted.

Ammi's cake? Yasmin heard ringing in her head.

Ammi's cake???

AMMI'S CAKE????

It was *her* cake, it was *her* birthday, and none of this was *her* fault. But would her parents listen to her side of the story? NO! And her aunties never helped, not to mention her horrible brothers.

A whole wave of noise came crashing down. Ammi was calling out an endless stream of orders. Papa was scooping up pieces of cake from the floor. Auntie Gigi and Auntie Bibi were trying to comfort Ammi and Yasmin's brothers were just licking bits of icing that had fallen on the table.

Yasmin might as well have not been there.

So she did what she was best at, and disappeared.

CHAPTER FIVE
Careful What You
Wish For

Yasmin raced up all four flights of stairs, face caked in cake, and slammed her door shut behind her.

She grabbed her pillow and started beating it up.

Her *stupid* THUMP! *brothers* THUD! *were always* THUMP! THUMP! *getting her into trouble* THWACK! THUMP! THUD!

Her family always blamed her for everything.

Wiping her face with a towel, she kicked off her shiny shoes and threw them at her cupboard, where they slammed against the wooden door. Jumping on to her bed, she buried her head in the pillow and tried to block out the sounds of Ammi's continued yells. It was no use. It was like there was a yodelling competition going on downstairs. She wanted nothing more than to stand on her bed, open her mouth and let out a roar so big that it would tear the whole house apart!

But . . . it wasn't worth it. Nobody would stop talking for long enough to listen to her..

Yasmin got up and walked over to her mirror. She looked into the glass with such a severe expression she nearly scared herself. Finally she closed her eyes and, with all the brain strength she could muster, she made a wish.

I wish I could stand up for myself.

With her eyes closed, she listened out to hear if the shouting downstairs had died down.

What she heard instead was a thud. Coming from inside the cupboard.

And another.

And another!

Yasmin stared at the cupboard door. Where was the knocking coming from?

The cupboard fell silent. The noise from downstairs now seemed muffled compared to

Yasmin's own heavy breathing. She reached out and carefully knocked once on the wooden cupboard door.

The air seemed to chill around her. After a moment, she heard the knocking coming from inside again. Against her better judgment, Yasmin banged harder.

The knocking from within the cupboard was louder this time. Something was definitely in there – a mouse or a rat? – but Yasmin couldn't ask her parents to come and investigate. She was still too angry with them.

She fetched her tennis racket from the corner of the room. Approaching the cupboard door on tiptoe, she closed her eyes, counted to three and then swung the cupboard open . . .

'Oi, love! I'm having a kip here. Your stomping woke me up!'

In blind panic, Yasmin swung the tennis racket in the direction of the noise.

'ARGH! WATCH IT!'

Yasmin slowly opened her eyes. She couldn't believe what she was seeing. It was, frankly, unbelievable.

'Didn't your mum ever tell you it's rude to smack people with tennis rackets?'

Yasmin blinked hard. Was there a *talking toy llama* in her cupboard?

'Hellooooo, anybody home?' the llama said.

Yasmin remained frozen to the spot.

'Right, well, I'm gonna give myself a tour of the house,' the llama said in a broad cockney accent, getting up out of the pile of old socks it seemed to have been using as a bed. Before it could escape, Yasmin slammed the door shut.

Was she dreaming? Just to be sure, she pinched herself. *Ouch!* She was definitely awake, and now her arm hurt. But she was pinching herself because there was a *talking toy llama* in her cupboard. And not just *any* talking toy llama. It was the gross toy llama from the market! It must have fallen out of her schoolbag earlier when she tossed it to the ground.

'All right love, tell you what. Open up the cupboard and I'll explain myself,' the llama said reasonably. 'I don't want no trouble.'

Tentatively, Yasmin opened the cupboard door just a crack. It felt like there was a swarm of angry bees in her stomach. She put her eye to the gap and

36

peered in.

The llama laughed. 'Come on!'

Yasmin opened the door an inch more.

'That's it, I don't bite.' The llama peered out at her. 'But I do spit!'

With amazing precision, the llama aimed a perfect spray of matted fur fluff through the crack in the door, hitting Yasmin right on the nose. Seizing the opportunity, he jumped out of the cupboard and on to the desk, knocking off all her schoolbooks.

The little trickster! Yasmin thought, wiping her face. I'll show him!

Grabbing her filled-to-the-brim laundry basket, Yasmin catapulted across the room with a trail of dirty clothes flying in her wake. She barrel-rolled across the bed like a cop in a Hollywood film and slammed the basket down, trapping the llama underneath.

'I *want* to be angry, but I'm actually quite

impressed,' the llama remarked from inside his new prison.

Yasmin looked at him gruffly, putting her heaviest maths textbooks on the top of the basket to keep it secure. She sat down on the bed to catch her breath and make sense of the situation.

'Wot?' the llama asked cheekily. 'Cat got your tongue?'

CHAPTER SIX
It's Llama Time!

Oh! I knew there was something I was supposed to mention. The cat did, in fact, have Yasmin's tongue. Though not literally. In a world of talking toy llamas, it's probably best I'm clear about that.

What I mean is, Yasmin didn't speak. Ever.

In the last seven years or so of her life, Yasmin had barely said a word. It's not that she didn't know how to speak; she did. It's just that she didn't want to, and for three very good reasons.

1: You've seen how loud her family is. It's a good thing this is a book and not a TV show, or you'd have a headache by the end.

2: When Yasmin first learned to speak, her brothers used it as yet another thing to tease her about. Every time she opened her mouth, they would burst into hysterics at the sound of her voice. They even started calling her Trombone which, if you've ever heard a Trombone, is a particularly unkind nickname.

3: *The Purple/Poo Incident.* To be discussed later.

So, Yasmin kept quiet. It's not as if anyone noticed. She would just have been another voice trying her best to be heard over the dinner table. If she was going to speak, she wanted to be heard. To make an impact. So, just as she'd got the hang of talking at three years old, she gave it up, and she hadn't looked back since.

Yasmin shook her head vigorously from side to side and let her eyes refocus. Nope, the llama was still there. Had she fallen over in the kitchen and banged her head? Was she having a weird dream?

'Look, look, look, I think we might have got off on the wrong foot back there,' said the llama. 'I'm Levi.

What's your name, love?'

Yasmin chewed at her lip nervously. If this was just a crazy dream she might as well go along with it. Maybe she'd snap out of it and wake up in bed. Cautiously, she picked up her schoolbag and pointed to her name written on the front.

'Yasmin, huh? Ya don't speak?'

Yasmin shook her head.

'Interesting . . .' Levi seemed to be mulling something over in his fluff-stuffed head. 'I don't blame ya for keepin' quiet. Best to keep yourself to yourself round these endz.'

Yasmin looked confused.

'These endz?' Levi prompted. 'It means *these streets*. Whitechapel ain't what it used to be. I've been living here for a while and even I don't recognise the place no more. There's more and more trendy young people in flashy clothes setting up coffee shops. I mean, how many coffee shops d'ya need?'

Yasmin couldn't work this all out. A talking toy llama from Whitechapel? She was quite sure that even real llamas didn't live in London, and certainly not in the heart of the East End. The most exotic thing she'd seen where she lived was a rat in the garden that turned orange after it ate a bag of cheese balls.

'How long you lived here? Twenty ... thirty years?' Levi enquired.

Yasmin snorted and hopped up on to her bed to reach her huge blackboard. Picking up some chalk she wrote: *I'm only ten! It's my birthday.*

'Then where are all yer presents? Yer parents must be cheapskates.'

It was true that Yasmin was a bit miffed with her rubbish logic puzzle book.

'What about your mates, they at least get you a card?'

Yasmin shook her head and wrote: *I don't have friends at school.*

'No mates, eh?' Levi raised an eyebrow. 'We'll have to sort that.'

The chalk was still firmly gripped in Yasmin's hand. This was really happening. This was real – a real pain in the butt! The last thing she needed now was another person – or llama – rabbiting on in her ear all the time. Maybe she could take him back to the bargain bucket? She might even get a refund.

But her thoughts were interrupted by a *thud, thud, thud,* coming up the stairs – the unmistakable sound of Ammi's footsteps. She was five floors below, but Yasmin's mother didn't exactly have a light step.

With her best stern expression, Yasmin hopped off the bed and mimed zipping her mouth shut to Levi.

'Eh?' he said. 'I ain't a mind reader!'

She rolled her eyes and put her finger to her lips.

'Ahhhhhh, you want me to shut it? Tough luck, princess! I think I should let that person know about you hitting me with tennis racket!' Levi laughed and stuck his tongue out at her.

How rude! Yasmin thought. Well, she could be rude too. She stomped up to the laundry bin and plonked her bum right down on top it, wiggling around for good measure.

'I can see you're a tough cookie to crack,' Levi yelled up at the bum that was holding him hostage. 'Well, I don't give up so easy either!'

At the top of his lungs (do toy llamas even have

LaLaLa Laaaaaa, it's Llama Time!

lungs?) he began singing, 'La la la laaaaaa, it's Llama Time!'

Yasmin chucked some pillows and her duvet on top of the basket to try and muffle the sound. Levi responded by running around inside, causing the pile to shake and tremble wildly.

What was she going to *do*? Ammi was already making her way up the last flight of stairs.

In desperation, Yasmin grabbed the laundry basket and threw it aside. Swiftly, she caught Levi, who kicked and wriggled around in her hands, and took him to the window.

'Oi, *oi*, ow! Let me go! You nasty little girl!'

He fought and fought but Yasmin held on tightly. Ammi's footsteps were getting ever closer. She silently hoped that Levi's teeth would be made of wool, just in case he decided to bite her.

With one hand tightly holding Levi, Yasmin opened her window.

'HEY! Don't you dare throw me out! There's

47

pigeons out there and they look angry!'

Yasmin held him out of the open window. And just as the bedroom door creaked open, she let go.

'WHATONEARTHAREYOUDOING?' Ammi's thick eyebrows were raised so high, they could have touched the ceiling. 'WHATSGOINGON WITHYOUCHILD?'

Motioning to the open window, Yasmin fanned her face to pretend that she was hot and puffed out her cheeks. Her bright red face made it all the more convincing.

'ITSAMESSINHERE!' Ammi yelled, picking through the chaos of Yasmin's usually spotless room. 'YOUHAVEBEENTHROWING ATANTRUM!'

Yasmin wanted to defend herself, but that would mean revealing that there had been a magic toy llama in her room. Or that she had gone totally bananas. She could feel her face flushing with frustration.

Ammi saw Yasmin's red cheeks as a sign of anger.

'HOWDAREYOUGETANGRYWITHME! INMYDAYCHILDRENRESPECTEDTHEIR PARENTS...'

Yasmin thought the best she could do to ease the situation was to start tidying her room and nodding from time to time to show she was listening.

'ANDAFTERYOURUINEDTHECAKE! WHATDID I DOTODESERVETHISNAUGHTYCHILD?'

Usually, if you let Ammi rant for long enough she began to run out of steam at around the eighteen-minute mark. But this time, Yasmin was saved by the bell. The telephone rang and immediately Papa was yelling up the stairs:

'Darling, answer the phone! I'm doing my evening sudoku!'

Ammi narrowed her eyes. 'WEWILLFINISHTHIS LATER.' Then she turned and stomped back downstairs.

The anger started to creep back into Yasmin's chest, making her face hot and her tummy tight.

She turned around, trying to stay calm, before it all bubbled up and she launched herself on to the bed, pummelling the mattress with her fists.

A voice came from outside the window. 'Wow, you can pack a punch.'

In all the ruckus, Yasmin had forgotten about Levi. She'd hoped she'd imagined him. Scrabbling up from the bed, she peeped out of the window.

'Down 'ere!'

Yasmin lowered her gaze. She saw Levi

hanging by his front two feet from the window ledge.

Fun fact: llamas don't have hooves. I know, I thought they did too, but actually, they are 'bump-footed'. They've got two toes with a bumpy pad underneath which is just *all kinds* of wrong.

With a huge groan Levi heaved himself up and on to the window ledge. 'Lucky I've been doing all them pull-ups at the gym.'

Yasmin made a grab for him but he dodged her, leaping through the air and landing on the bed.

'Whoa, don't worry, I ain't going downstairs.' Levi padded about in a circle and then curled up on the duvet. 'I only said that earlier to wind you up.'

Yasmin faceplanted on to the bed.

'Besides, you're the only one who can hear me talk or see me move. So, I think we should be mates,' he said, settling down.

What did he mean she was the only one? Surely such a loudmouth llama could be heard by everyone?

'Nope, just you,' Levi confirmed. 'Now, be a doll and tidy up. It's a mess in here.'

Yasmin reached out and whacked him off the bed.

Yep. This was *no ordinary day*.

'Michael?'

'Good morning, Miss Zainab.'

'Jeremiah?'

'Here, Miss Zainab.'

'Betty?'

'Morning, Miss Zainab.'

'Tia?'

'Good morning, Miss Zainab.'

'Yasmin?'

. . .

Miss Zainab looked up from her desk and Yasmin blinked back at her. She hadn't slept much, spending most of the night convinced she was in a llama-infested nightmare. She'd only managed to get dressed and leave for school by keeping Levi

54

trapped underneath the laundry basket and shoving a heavy duvet over the top to drown out his chatter. It had been exhausting.

'And Yasmin's . . . here.' Miss Zainab smiled. 'Great, a full class. Plus, our new addition.'

Standing dutifully next to Miss Zainab's desk was a boy. A new boy. He was quite tall for his age, skinny, with tight curly black hair. Without any prompting he suddenly stood forward.

'Hi! I'm Ezra.'

He looked expectantly around the room. A girl at the back of the class, Tia, sniggered. Tia had been Yasmin's best friend in Years One and Two, but as soon as they came back from summer holiday for Year Three Tia decided they couldn't be friends any more.

'It's just . . . you don't *speak*, Yasmin.' Tia had shrugged. 'And me and the other girls think it's a bit weird . . .' Then she'd turned and run off in the direction of the group of girls and hadn't looked back since.

Now that same group of girls were giggling at Ezra from the back of the classroom. Clearly, they thought *he* was weird too. Ezra didn't seem to notice. He was engrossed in the Rubik's Cube Miss Zainab had on her desk.

'Ezra is joining our class –'

Miss Zainab took the Rubik's Cube out of Ezra's hand. He picked up a mechanical pencil and started clicking away at it.

'– and I expect everyone –'

Miss Zainab removed the pencil and Ezra immediately walked over to the check out the wall display.

'– to give him a warm welcome!'

Miss Zainab finally caught hold of Ezra's hand and led him back to the front of the class. He just couldn't seem to keep still.

'So,' Miss Zainab said. 'Who would like to be a buddy for Ezra this week as he gets used to the school?'

Yasmin's kindly teacher was met with a resounding silence. Yasmin certainly wasn't going to volunteer. She couldn't look after someone new whilst also trying to work out what to do with Levi. Yasmin did her best to avoid her teacher's gaze, looking firmly down at her desk. Until . . .

'Yasmin!' Miss Zainab chirped. Yasmin winced. 'You will be the perfect person to buddy up with Ezra. You're so sensible and . . . focused. Plus, you know what it's like to be a new student.'

To a chorus of giggles from Tia and the other girls, Miss Zainab pulled up an empty chair next to Yasmin's desk and plonked an exercise book down on it. Ezra happily strolled over and shuffled in next to Yasmin, smiling a gap-tooth smile at her all the while.

Yasmin grimaced. This was only going to make her life a thousand times harder. Couldn't she get some peace anywhere?

But Miss Zainab was right. Yasmin did know what it's like to be a new student. And this, dear reader, is where the infamous Purple/Poo Incident comes in. (I know you've been desperate to hear about it since I mentioned it earlier.) So let's pop over to:

MEMORY CORNER

I would briefly like to take you back in time to Yasmin's first day at Fish Lane Primary School.

Awwwww! She was so little and cute. Except that this was quite possibly the most embarrassing day of her life – and luckily for us, the funniest.

Picture the scene. It's a whole school assembly. Yasmin doesn't know anyone. The headteacher calls her up in front of everyone to introduce herself. Yasmin, who last spoke when she was three years old, decides that today's the day she tries speaking again.

The headteacher starts easy. She prompts, 'Tell everyone your name.'

Yasmin gulps, coughs a little and then announces quietly, 'Yasmin.'

Then the headteacher throws a curveball – something Yasmin hasn't prepared for.

'And why don't you tell us something you like, for example . . . your favourite colour?'

Yasmin's throat goes dry. She likes purple and

blue. But she's only just conquered saying one word. She isn't about to say three. She racks her brain.

Purple or blue?

Purple or blue?

PURPLE OR BLUE?

Then in a confident, somewhat too loud, voice Yasmin declares: 'Poo!'

There is an audible silence in the hall.

Instead of saying purple *or* blue, she ends up squashing the words together! Mortified, Yasmin runs back to her place with her head low, trying not to show everyone her burning red cheeks.

So . . . that had gone well. Not.

Yasmin, once again, had been reminded that speaking wasn't for her.

It's safe to say that that memory was one she was trying to forget.

CHAPTER EIGHT
One More Probllama

It was breaktime and, as usual, Yasmin was sitting at a desk inside practising checkers. Her opponent was incredibly tough. She seemed to know Yasmin's every move. But this was probably because she was playing against herself.

You see, not many other ten-year-olds liked playing checkers – a strategy board game where two players moved their counters diagonally across the black and white squares to capture each other's pieces. It took patience, forward-thinking . . . and was most commonly played by those aged seventy or over.

Yasmin didn't really have any friends at school, especially after the Purple/Poo Incident and Tia branding her 'weird'. She had been upset at first, but now she was kind of used to it. If she could find a ten-year-old who didn't mind one-sided conversations, knew that checkers and draughts were *not* the same thing, and loved jammy dodgers, then that would be perfect. But for now, she would stay inside at break, practising at every opportunity for her upcoming matches.

Unfortunately, she wasn't the only one who had decided to sit inside this breaktime. At the far side of the classroom, Ezra was perched on one of the red plastic chairs in the reading corner. He was surrounded by at least ten books which he continually picked up, put down and then moved on to the next. He must have felt Yasmin looking over, because he suddenly perked up and caught her eye.

'Oh, hi Yasmin!' He gave Yasmin another big toothy grin. (Well, both of his front teeth were missing but you get the picture.) Yasmin immediately pretended to focus on her checkers game.

'Do you always stay in at breaktime?' Ezra questioned, moving over to Yasmin's table.

Now that she'd made eye contact, it was clear that Ezra thought she wanted to be friends. This certainly wouldn't do. Yasmin made a mental note to be more aloof in the future.

(I thought I'd just pop in to say here that aloof is one of my favourite words. It means cool and distant, but I just like the way it sounds. *Aloooooooooooof*. If you say it over and over again really fast, it starts to sound like *floof*. Am I rambling? Sorry.)

Ezra picked up Yasmin's pencil case, fiddling with the glitter on the lettering. 'Miss Zainab told me you don't speak. I get it. My brother doesn't speak either . . . but I suppose he is only three months old.'

Yasmin flushed red. Why did Miss Zainab have to pair Ezra with her? Couldn't she have chosen one of the other boys? Playing checkers at breaktime was Yasmin's way of relaxing – something she desperately needed after a stressful morning of pretending there wasn't a talking toy llama in her bedroom.

Ezra turned his attention to the game Yasmin was strategising. 'Oh!' he exclaimed. 'You're playing checkers!'

Yasmin raised her eyebrows in surprise. Ezra was the first child she had ever met who actually knew what checkers was (apart from her brothers, who knew just enough to tease her about it).

Ezra picked up the white piece and completed a move that Yasmin had been planning out. He chuckled as he took away the black piece. 'I always play against my granddad when we go to visit him in Jamaica. My mum said it would help me learn to focus. Apparently I have a short concentration span . . . but I'm actually just very interested in lots of things at the same time.'

Yasmin picked up the black piece, making two swift moves that ended the game.

Ezra whistled. 'Wow, you're good! Hey, we should

play together!'

Yasmin started to pack the pieces away. She did not want to play against Ezra. In fact she was hoping that any minute she'd wake up, and both he and this whole Levi thing would be a dream.

'Don't you want to play again?' Ezra offered. 'Lunch isn't over for a few minutes and I don't fancy going outside. It's just too loud out there, you know?'

Yasmin did know. She often wanted to go outside and play with the other children, but all the ruckus made her head spin. It reminded her too much of home. If *she* found it hard to focus, then Ezra must have found it impossible.

The school bell rang, abruptly ending Yasmin and Ezra's non-conversation. Ezra sighed and started getting out his pencils. Yasmin did feel a bit bad, but it wasn't her fault that Miss Zainab had paired Ezra with her. She should have chosen one of the more sociable children.

Yasmin looked around at her classmates, who were all settling down in their chairs. Maybe she could convince someone to take Ezra off her hands? That would be one less probllama in her life.

Perhaps last night had just been a figment of her imagination. Perhaps when she returned home, the laundry basket in her bedroom would be empty and Levi gone.

'Okay class, let's begin fifth period with ten minutes of silent reading.' Miss Zainab got out a huge pile of exercise books and thudded them down on her table to mark.

Yasmin got out her reading book: a non-fiction book about life in Roman times.

'PSHT! YASMIN!'

She dropped the book. Peeping down at her bookbag, she kicked it open to reveal . . .

'Guess who!?'

Levi winked. Yasmin gasped.

Miss Zainab looked up from her desk. Yasmin

quickly gave her an apologetic smile. After a frozen moment, she looked down again.

Levi was jumping at her ankles. 'Can we hang out? I was well bored at home.'

Yasmin put her finger to her lips and gave Levi a hard stare. It was hard to believe she was the only one who could hear him or see him move, but no one around her seemed to have noticed the noise coming from under her desk. Not even Ezra, who was sitting right next to her.

There was no way that Yasmin was letting Levi get her into trouble at school, especially not in her favourite teacher's class. She picked up her book again, but her hands were too sweaty to hold it. Her heart was beating a mile a minute.

'Ow!' shouted Tia from the back of the class. 'Someone chucked a rubber at me!'

Miss Zainab's eyes narrowed. 'Who did that?'

No one put their hand up. With a sneaking suspicion, Yasmin reached down into her bag and

looked inside her pencil case. Sure enough, her rubber was missing. Levi winked at her.

'Miss Zainab.' Tia looked Yasmin right in the eye. 'It has Yasmin's name written on it.'

Yasmin clenched her fist and cursed her good organisation skills. She would never write her name

on a rubber again.

'Yasmin, did you throw the rubber?' Miss Zainab asked calmly.

Yasmin shook her head.

'Perhaps it was an accident.' Miss Zainab picked the rubber up and gave it back to Yasmin. 'Let's make sure it doesn't happen again, hmmn? Back to reading please, everyone.'

Tia glared suspiciously at Yasmin before turning back to her book.

Yasmin breathed a small sigh of relief. She kicked the bag Levi was hiding in.

There was no response.

She hurriedly searched the bag, but it was no use. Levi wasn't in there.

This could only be bad news.

'Argh! Miss Zainab!' Tia shrieked again. 'Yasmin threw something else at me!'

Miss Zainab slammed her pen down on the desk. 'Oh, for goodness' sake. How can you be so sure it was Yasmin?'

Yasmin wasn't looking at her teacher. She was hurriedly scanning the room for any trace of a toy llama.

'Because it's from that stupid game she plays,' said Tia with a pout, rubbing her head.

Yasmin suddenly spotted Levi perched on the desk behind Tia, the small cloth bag of checker pieces by his side.

'I got her right in the noggin!' He laughed in delight. 'She won't be telling on you no more!'

Miss Zainab stormed up to Tia's desk and inspected the missile. 'Yasmin Shah,' she said. 'I know you had a falling out with Tia, but there is no need to disrupt the class.' She shook her head. 'Really, you've left me no choice but to give you a detention.'

'Whoops.' Levi lowered his tail between his legs. 'I didn't mean for *that* to happen . . . I just thought things could do with a little shake-up.'

Yasmin felt tears brimming in her eyes. Her first detention! How would she ever tell Ammi and Papa? She screwed her fist up and banged it on the table. That stupid llama!

'Just tell her it wasn't you, Yasmin!' Levi urged, jumping up and down on the table.

Yasmin turned away angrily, determined not to cry.

'What a shame, Yasmin. You had a perfect record . . .' Miss Zainab returned to her desk and wrote down Yasmin's name in the detention logbook.

Under the table, Yasmin could feel Levi wriggling back into her rucksack. She resisted the urge to boot him across the classroom.

'Well . . .' His voice floated up to her sheepishly. 'There's a first time for everything, innit?'

CHAPTER NINE
Secret Agent Yasmin

Operation 'Get Rid of Levi' was a go. Within one day he'd managed to give Yasmin her first detention in the history of ever, and she wasn't about to wait around and see what further shenanigans he had in store.

Luckily, Miss Zainab had agreed to a short lunchtime detention, since Yasmin had a clean track record. As soon as she got home, Yasmin locked Levi in her cupboard (not without a struggle first) and began planning.

It was time to give Levi the boot. And she knew JUST how to do it . . .

She had never actually acted out one of her missions before. But, like Levi said, there was a first time for everything.

The Adventures of Secret Agent Yasmin

7.45am – Yasmin and Ammi leave for school in T minus 60 seconds.

BACKPACK

ILLEGAL CONTRABAND

WALL SCALING DEVICE

MISSING RATIONS

TOP SECRET NUCLEAR EQUATIONS

3 minutes later . . .

7.45am – Everything is in place. Secret Agent Yasmin waits for the perfect moment.

Release the secret weapon.

Just in time!

Whoosh!

CHAPTER TEN
A Load of Rubbish

'YASMINSHAHYOUAREINBIGTROUBLE!'

A voice came booming from the school gate at the end of the day. Although there was a crowd of parents blocking her view, Yasmin recognised that voice instantly.

She had spent the day checking her schoolbag every ten seconds to make sure that Levi hadn't materialised out of nowhere. But it seemed like her first ever mission-in-action had worked. Levi had disappeared, hopefully into a big pile of rubbish somewhere. So why was she in trouble? The school didn't ring parents about lunchtime detentions.

It must have been something else. *Something worse.*

As Yasmin walked towards the school gate, she

could feel the eyes of every parent in the playground on her. They knew just as well as she did that Yasmin was in for a long rant. Ammi's rants were famous throughout the neighbourhood.

But, unusually, there was no rant. For the whole journey back to 11 Fish Lane, Ammi refused to tell Yasmin what she had done wrong. She marched angrily ahead, occasionally turning around to shout, 'HURRY UP!' before turning back and storming onwards. It actually sent shivers up Yasmin's spine to think of what might have rendered Ammi (almost) speechless.

On they went – past the butcher's, past the corner shop and around the corner. Ammi stomped so loudly, Yasmin was sure that the cobbled streets of Brick Lane would crack under her feet. Mean Mrs Robinson from number 42, carrying a pint of semi-skimmed milk, caught Yasmin's eye and gave her a look that seemed to say, 'I know what you've done . . .'

Yasmin racked her brain. What on earth was

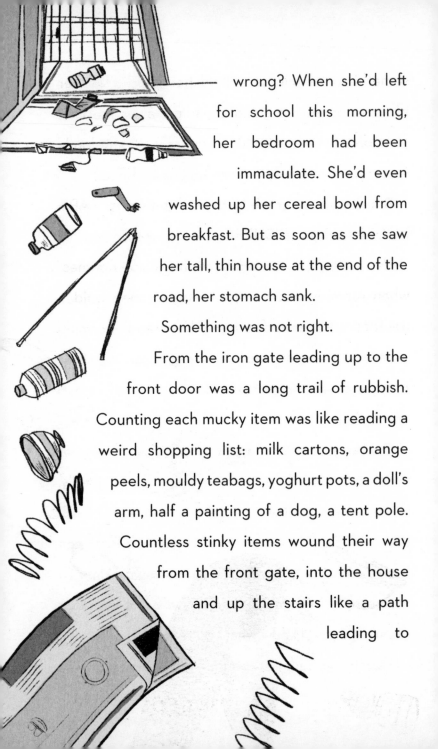

wrong? When she'd left for school this morning, her bedroom had been immaculate. She'd even washed up her cereal bowl from breakfast. But as soon as she saw her tall, thin house at the end of the road, her stomach sank.

Something was not right.

From the iron gate leading up to the front door was a long trail of rubbish. Counting each mucky item was like reading a weird shopping list: milk cartons, orange peels, mouldy teabags, yoghurt pots, a doll's arm, half a painting of a dog, a tent pole. Countless stinky items wound their way from the front gate, into the house and up the stairs like a path leading to something. Yasmin scratched her head. Had her brothers pulled a prank that had gone wrong? Had someone broken into their house and randomly sprayed rubbish everywhere?

Ammi stopped at the bottom of the stairs. 'PAPA YOURDAUGHTERISHERE!'

Now Yasmin was *really* confused. Sometimes when Ammi was too angry to speak, she would get Papa to do it for her. That was usually for the best because an angry Ammi could trigger a volcanic eruption. But why was Ammi angry with *her* that the house was a mess? A thought suddenly popped into Yasmin's head. She quickly shook it away.

No, he's gone. He must be!

Papa poked his head out of the kitchen. He beckoned Yasmin to follow him. With her head full of questions, she followed him in a daze. They walked up two flights of stairs, trying not to slip on the crisp packets and newspapers strewn around.

When they got to her parents' room, Auntie Bibi and Auntie Gigi were waiting for them, towering over Papa who was sitting on the edge of the bed. He patted beside him for Yasmin to sit and the aunties simultaneously raised their eyebrows at Yasmin. It was a look that said, *'You're in for it now.'*

'I am a simple man, Yasmin. I do not ask for much from you,' Papa sighed in what must have been the understatement of the century. 'I only wish for the respect and obedience of my youngest child. But *this* has gone too far.'

Yasmin's mouth dropped open. They thought that *she* had done this? She shook her head frantically and got out her notepad to write a message.

'We know it was you, Yasmin,' Papa explained. 'The trail leads all the way to your bedroom. And Ammi said she saw you out by the rubbish truck this morning.'

Yasmin let out a sigh of desperation. So much for being a secret agent. But she hadn't made the mess! She wanted to defend herself, but how could she explain any of it?

'Perhaps she is becoming a teenager already. Perhaps this is a rebellious phase,' Auntie Bibi said to Papa, as if Yasmin wasn't even there.

'It's true, Brother, she has been acting strangely recently,' Auntie Gigi agreed.

Yasmin screwed up her fists, *The aunties were making things worse!*

Papa looked even more disappointed. 'A

rebellious teenager . . . This may be hard to believe, Yasmin, but I have not always been such a shining example of respectability. I, too, went through a naughty phase as a child. Your aunties said we should forbid you from playing checkers as punishment, but I want to give you another chance. I was able to turn my behaviour around, and you will too. Starting with cleaning the entire house, top to bottom!'

Yasmin felt like crying. She didn't need to turn her behaviour around. She *was* a good daughter! But trying to argue with her parents, especially when the aunties were egging them on, would simply make matters worse.

Dejected, she nodded and kissed Papa on the cheek. He grunted and patted her on the head. As much as he tried to be the 'man of the house', even Papa couldn't stay angry after a kiss. Yasmin didn't even look her Aunties or Ammi in the eye. She simply turned and trudged up the stairs wondering how her life had taken such a turn for the worse in a matter of days.

As she marched through her brothers' room, they started clapping.

'Well done, Yasmin! Your first prank!' Tall Brother said admiringly.

Short Brother laughed. 'You're becoming just like us. I'm almost proud.'

Yasmin ignored them. She had a pretty good idea who was behind this, although she desperately hoped it wasn't true. A sinking feeling washed over her as she took the stairs up to her room. With each step her stomach dropped further, until she felt quite sick with worry.

She took a deep breath and threw her bedroom door open.

And there, sitting on her bed, was Levi.

CHAPTER ELEVEN
The Comeback Llama

All the confusion and worry that Yasmin had felt suddenly turned into rage. She picked up the nearest object, which happened to be a toy truck, and hurled it at Levi. It missed.

Levi put his book down and lowered his glasses. 'Ah, Yasmin,' he said. 'I didn't see you there.'

Yasmin grabbed the next truck.

'There's no need for that,' Levi announced. 'I can see you're angry. Let me explain.'

Yasmin wasn't angry. She was *livid*. How had this stupid thing found its way back to her? He should be on top of a rubbish tip right now! She picked up the small plastic bin in her room, tipped out the contents and pointed it at Levi.

'First of all, put that thing down, 'cos I ain't getting in it!' Levi said. 'I'm the one angry with you! You plonked me in the rubbish. So I taught you a lesson in return.'

Yasmin furiously started picking up all the bits of rubbish lying around and hurling them at Levi, one by one. First a soggy bread roll, then a ketchup-covered apple, followed by anything she could find!

'Calm down!' Levi yelped, dodging a flying half-eaten biscuit. 'Your aim is terrible!'

Yasmin stopped chucking the rubbish at him and caught her breath.

'Don't you even wanna know how I got back?' Levi sounded almost excited to share this with her. 'As soon as I was taken out of that truck and was shoved in that rubbish pile, I planned my escape.'

Frustrated, Yasmin flopped down on the floor. She'd been outsmarted by a toy who had stuffing where his brain should be.

'You see, I got connections,' Levi said. 'There's a rat in the rubbish tip that owed me a favour.'

Yasmin furrowed her brow. Was he kidding?

'Let's just say, I saved his marriage. Managed to sort him out a nice hunk of cheese for his wife's birthday.'

Eeww. Yasmin did not need the rat visuals.

'Anyway, he sorted an escape route, round the back of the tip where they park the trucks. He told me when the next truck was leaving so I just hopped on and rode it back here to your house. Brought a few presents with me an' all.' He winked at the piles of rubbish.

Yasmin wrote on her chalkboard. *Not cool.*

'Well. listen up and take notice. You can't get rid of me,' Levi continued more seriously, 'as hard as you – OOF!'

Yasmin had lunged forward and grabbed Levi. She had *really* run out of patience. It was going to take her hours to clear up this mess, and it wasn't even *her* fault. She didn't want her parents to be angry with her. She wanted them to *believe* her – she wasn't naughty!.

Yasmin suddenly realised she was gripping Levi rather too tightly. She narrowed her eyes at him.

Levi gulped. 'Uh oh.'

There was no point wallowing. Yasmin needed to be *proactive*. She would make the house cleaner than ever before. Prove that she wasn't turning into a 'moody teenager'. But first . . .

Yasmin rushed down the stairs with Levi still in

her fist, and peered into Auntie Gigi and Auntie Bibi's room. They were both at the salon, having their yearly toenail clipping.

She knew the perfect place to put Levi for punishment. In her aunties' wardrobe was a drawer where they stored all their old underwear. They never threw anything away, so the pants just stayed there in the dark, getting mouldier and mustier by the day.

Yasmin opened the deep drawer in Auntie Bibi's wardrobe and shoved Levi far down inside, underneath all the enormous old pants.

'Noooooooooooo!' he yelled.

She slammed it shut. Now she couldn't hear his yells at all, as they were muffled by multiple pairs of parachute-sized knickers and huge bras. She smirked. That would teach him a lesson. And since Levi didn't come alive in front of anyone else, it would keep him quiet for a while too.

After what felt like a lifetime, Yasmin finally cleared up Levi's mess. She even scrubbed the floors and polished the stairs so that they were as shiny as a penny. Auntie Gigi was so impressed, she gave Yasmin a lolly to say well done. Her parents gave her a nod of approval.

Wearily, Yasmin climbed up the four flights of stairs to her room and got straight into bed. She'd never been this exhausted in her entire life. At least in here, she was by herself. The only sanctuary of peace she had in her life. No way was Levi ever going to share it with her. No. Way.

If Levi wouldn't leave by himself, then she would *make* him.

She lay in bed, her tired mind busy with the events of the last couple of days. It was all making her brain feel very muddled. She was on thin ice with her parents, and who knew what Levi planned next?

The thought made Yasmin squirm under the covers. She sighed. Perhaps she needed to confront Levi. What did he *really* want from her?

To clear her head, Yasmin used the trick that always helped her get to sleep. She closed her eyes and imagined herself at the elderly people's daycentre, sitting at the checkers table, making the winning move and being handed the championship trophy. Everyone would be clapping, and her parents would be so proud! The trophy would have her name carved at the bottom on a plaque, and she could bring it to school for show and tell! Well, maybe just the *show* part.

Yasmin smiled to herself at this thought, and fell asleep.

CHAPTER TWELVE
The Best Worst Day of the Week

It was a beautiful sunny morning *and* a Friday. This was the best day of the week – and not just because the teachers were always in a better mood. On Friday afternoons, Yasmin went to the elderly people's daycentre to play checkers.

On this particular Friday, Yasmin awoke to the sound of what was either a cat exploding after it had eaten some bagpipes, *or* Auntie Bibi screaming. Something told her that Levi *might* have found his way out of the knicker drawer. Oops . . .

She quickly jumped out of bed and put on her dressing gown. If she was just sensible and remained calm, maybe Ammi and Papa would be calm too.

But, as she walked down the stairs into her brothers' room, remaining calm wasn't really an option. Instead, Yasmin burst out laughing. Tall Brother was staggering around the room with one of Auntie Bibi's humongous pink bras strapped over his eyes. They bulged out strangely, making him look like a human-sized fly. Short Brother had a black lacy bra strapped over his head, covering his ears and making him look like a monkey, if monkeys had ears made of bras.

'You'll pay for this!' Short Brother cursed as he tried in vain to

remove his black lacy monkey ears.

On top of her brothers' TV, Yasmin saw two fluffy ears appear, followed by Levi's head.

'Wotcha think?' he snorted. 'I caught them in the middle of the night setting up a prank outside your room, so thought I'd turn the tables on 'em, the rotters.'

As long as this was the extent of his antics, Yasmin could forgive Levi. She might even thank him eventually, for giving her brothers a taste of their own medicine.

Levi hopped from the TV to the bed and up into the pocket of Yasmin's dressing gown, right under her brother's noses. 'Wait till you see what I did in your aunties' room. You're gonna laugh y o u r pants off!'

Uh oh.

Yasmin hurried down the stairs to their room, bracing herself for whatever that fleabag Levi had got up to in the night.

As she entered the room, both of her aunties were sitting on the bed shaking their heads. Ammi and Papa both looked at Yasmin sternly, neither one saying a word. Instead, Ammi pointed at the mirror where Auntie Gigi did her makeup every morning. There, in her best red lipstick (a shade called Cherry Explosion) was written in big letters:

AUNTIE BIBI SMELLS OF WEE WEE

(auntie gigi smells too)

How childish! Yasmin grabbed her pocket and squeezed Levi tight.

'Ouch!' he wheezed. 'Why ain't you laughing? I thought it was well funny.'

He wasn't even sorry. Yasmin fetched a notepad and pen from the nightstand and hurriedly scribbled: *I didn't write that. I was asleep in my room all night!*

Auntie Gigi cocked an eyebrow, 'So who was it then?'

Yasmin's eyes shifted from side to side. What was she supposed to say? It was the magical toy llama in her pocket?

'ANDITWASN'TYOURBROTHERSEITHER!' Ammi cut in.

'Who is it that puts my lipstick on for me in the mornings, hm? I don't think your brothers even know what a lipstick looks like!' Auntie Gigi fumed.

It was true. Yasmin *did* have to apply her auntie's lipstick for her. Auntie Gigi refused to wear glasses since they didn't go with her style. Yasmin was the

95

only other person who knew where the lipsticks were kept.

'You're in big trouble!' Auntie Gigi continued. 'That was my best lipstick, and now it's ruined. To make matters worse, they've stopped making that one. Where am I supposed to get my Cherry Explosion now? It's just a Cherry Explosion all over the mirror!'

Papa pitched in. 'I thought I made myself clear, Yasmin. You've let me down.'

'YOUHAVELETUSALLDOWN!' Ammi added.

'Hang on a minute,' Levi piped up from inside her pocket. 'This wasn't your fault. Just write them a note and explain.'

Yasmin shot him a hard look. Explain what?

'Sorry Yasmin. I was just trying to back you up. The aunties were well annoyed yesterday, getting your dad all worked up like that.' Levi hung his head.

Yasmin shoved him down further inside her pocket. There were too many voices in the room!

'She must learn her manners. And there's only one person who can teach her *proper* manners,' Auntie Bibi warned.

This was bad. Yasmin knew who she was talking about. The strictest lady in the whole world. Her grandma, Daadi.

'I will be the judge of –' Papa began, puffing out his chest.

'Bibi is right, little brother,' Auntie Gigi chimed in. 'Mum will be a good influence on Yasmin. She should go and stay with her in Pakistan for the summer.'

'Come on girl, are you gonna let them punish you for nothing?' Levi scrabbled up from the depths of the pocket. 'Stand up for yourself! You deserve to be heard.'

This was really, *really* bad. Sent away to Pakistan for the summer? She would lose her own room, her Fridays at the elderly people's daycentre *and* miss the checkers tournament final!

Yasmin pleaded silently with Ammi. Ammi was

the only one who could save her now.

'As the head of this household, I will be the one to decide how Yasmin is punished.' Papa was wagging a finger at his two older sisters. 'To send Yasmin to Pakistan will cost money, and we haven't prepared for that. *However,* all children should learn the importance of obedience and good manners. And another thing –'

'ENOUGH,' Ammi bellowed.

The whole room fell silent. It was clear to all who was the head of this household.

Ammi put her hands on her hips. 'YASMINIS USUALLYGOOD.' She moved closer. 'SOSHEHAS ONE.MORE.CHANCE.'

CHAPTER THIRTEEN
Disgustingly Cute

Ammi's words rang around in Yasmin's head, filling her with dread. *One more chance.* That would be fine if she didn't have a talking toy llama following her around like a chirpy ghost.

Levi had threatened to pull another rubbish trick if Yasmin didn't take him with her to school, so she'd hidden him in her schoolbag where at least she could keep an eye on him. As she followed her older brothers to school (they had made a rule that she had to walk exactly five steps behind them at all times) Yasmin let her schoolbag whack against the wall.

'Oof. Ooh. Ouch!' Levi moaned. 'I was just trying to help you back there. Those old bats are always bossing you about!'

Yasmin zipped the bag shut tightly.

'Does that mean you're angry with me?' Levi's muffled voice came from inside.

Of course she was angry. He'd got her into trouble twice in the space of twenty-four hours! Yasmin took a deep breath and lifted her head high. If she was going to get through today, she would have to show Levi who was in charge.

At breaktime, Yasmin found a good spot on the carpet. All throughout English class Levi had been rustling around in her bag, trying to get comfortable. Yasmin had to give him a kick, which Miss Zainab caught, prompting Yasmin to give her teacher an 'everything's great here' smile. Miss Zainab had just seemed perplexed.

But at least now everyone else was outside. Everyone, that is, but Ezra.

'There you are!' He beamed. 'Right where I thought I'd find you.'

Yasmin inwardly groaned. Couldn't she get a

moment of peace? She lived in a house full of drama queens and drama llamas, plus now she had to look after Ezra too? Besides, she was a rubbish ally to have at school – she had no other friends. Surely Ezra would eventually find her 'weird', just like Tia did.

Ezra pulled up a chair and looked around for a toy to fiddle with. 'No checkers today?' he asked.

Yasmin suddenly realised that she had just been staring at the wall, going over and over what had happened that morning in her head.

'Something must be wrong.' Ezra had found a Slinky and was tossing it against the wall. 'Are you okay?'

'She's got a dodgy stomach, so I'd watch out if I were you!' shouted Levi.

He had escaped from her bag and was now posing stiffly on the bookshelf. Yasmin flinched. She was sure that Ezra must have heard *that*. Yep, he was definitely going to think she was weird.

Ezra followed Yasmin's gaze. 'What's up?'

He wandered over to the bookshelf and picked up Levi. He pulled a face. 'Eurgh . . . It's disgusting,' he decided after giving Levi a good checking over.

Yasmin motioned to Ezra to pass the pest over. She didn't want Levi pulling any tricks and getting her into trouble again.

'Oh sorry, is it yours?' Ezra handed Levi over. 'I meant, it's disgusting . . . ly . . . cute!'

Yasmin sniggered and shook her head. She stuck her tongue out and made a face of disgust at Levi.

Ezra looked relieved that he hadn't offended her. 'So how about we play that checkers game?' he said with a smile.

Yasmin hesitated, but figured that one game couldn't hurt. She nodded and stuffed Levi back in her bag.

'Great! I'll go get them.' Ezra smiled. 'Wait till I tell my grandad I've been playing checkers with a friend. He won't believe it!'

Yasmin let a small, surprised smile curl at her lips. Ezra had called her a *friend*.

Suddenly the classroom door to the playground opened and a boy from their class popped his head through. 'Hey, Ezra! We need someone else for our five-a-side team. Can you join?'

'Yeah sure!' Forgetting he was supposed to be fetching the checkers, Ezra ran towards the sunshine. As he got to the door, he paused. 'Oh, wait. Yasmin, do you want to come?'

The smile had already dropped off Yasmin's face. She shook her head.

'Okay. See ya later.' Ezra waved and disappeared.

Yasmin sat for a moment in silence.

She should have known he'd lose interest. And this was better anyway . . . Now she could remain focused on winning the checkers tournament and getting rid of Levi.

Yasmin nodded as if confirming with herself.

It was easier to be alone.

CHAPTER FOURTEEN
The Octogenarians' London Daycentre

WARNING! You are about to encounter an extreeeeeeeeeemely long word. However, I trust you, reader, and I know that we can get through this.

All together now!

Oct – o – gen – a – ri – an.

Phew. I need a lie-down.

Yasmin walked to the Octogenarians' London Daycentre (OLD for short) that afternoon with a heavy heart *and* a heavy bag, as Levi had decided to come along.

If you're wondering what an octogenarian is by the way, it isn't a machine that generates an octopus, like Yasmin thought. Although that would be cool. Octogenarian means someone who is in their eighties. This means that to attend OLD you had to be *old*. At least eighty, to be precise. This was a strict rule that Mr Patel from number 4 Fish Lane constantly grumbled about. He had wanted to attend OLD for years, but since he was currently only seventy-nine and three quarters, there was no way they were letting him in. There were members of OLD who were over the age of eighty-nine, but no one had the heart to kick them out, so they were allowed to stay as long as they didn't try and boss the younger members around.

Yasmin was by far the youngest 'member' of OLD. As a School Representative, she went to OLD once a week to learn about local history, and then write a report on what she learned. Although she wasn't learning as much about local history as she was about teaching the members how to use their mobiles. But the octogenarians liked having her there, she livened up the place a little, and she liked being there to listen to them. They didn't expect anything of her.

'Ugh. Wot are we doing 'ere?' Levi groaned as they entered the sitting room. 'No, no, no. These people are too old for you! We need kids! Kids are fun! Didn't you like playing pranks on your brothers?'

Yasmin supposed the prank with the bras *had* been quite funny. She walked over to the big leather armchair where she knew her best friend Miss Gillian (or Gilly, as she liked to be called) would be sitting.

Today, Gilly looked like a unicorn had thrown up on her. Her bright cardigan was multi-coloured and covered in glitter. Underneath she wore an even brighter lime green dress with 'PEACE AND LOVE' written across the front in big, shiny letters.

Levi whistled, peeping out at Gilly through a gap in the backpack. 'She might be old, but she knows how to dress,' he said.

'Yasmin! There's my quiet little mouse!' Gilly exclaimed. 'Thank God you're here. This lot bore me to death.'

Yasmin gave Gilly a big hug.

'You'll never guess what a silly sausage I was this morning,' said Gilly. 'I was sitting down to my cereal and I thought it tasted a lot sweeter than usual. I thought blimey, cornflakes have changed their recipe . . . Anyway, to cut a long story short, I'd mixed up the cartons and put custard on instead of milk! Mind you, it tasted quite good. I reckon I'll have custard again tomorrow . . .'

Yasmin listened with a smile on her face. She liked Gilly's stories, even if Gilly repeated them more than once.

'Bo-ring,' Levi sang, popping his head out of her bag. 'Aren't you tired of listening to her blab on?'

I'm tired of listening to YOU blab on, Yasmin thought, pushing her bag behind the sofa.

'Do you know who you're playing today?' Gilly

asked, cutting through Yasmin's thoughts.

It was Yasmin's fourth match in the checkers tournament that afternoon. She shook her head.

'He's a tough opponent, knows his stuff, a real hard player. He's over there.' Gilly pointed to an elderly gentleman who shakily picked up his cup of tea, took a sip and then immediately dropped it on the floor. All the other OLD members cheered. They loved a bit of action.

'Blimey, this place could do with some livening up.'

Yasmin tried to ignore Levi.

'Not the tea-dropper. The fella behind him,' Gilly said.

Behind the first man was another elderly gentleman. He had a thin, curly moustache and was wearing a stripy suit. Yasmin knew at once that a man with such a thin moustache could not be trusted.

'He tried to take my dessert the other day,' Gilly

whispered.

A sneaky, dessert-stealing moustache. It was time to take him down, Yasmin thought.

Levi wiggled his tiny tufts of eyebrows. 'Well, well, well,' he said. 'An oldie showdown – this might be fun after all.'

Yasmin said a silent prayer that Levi would stay put. At least just for half an hour.

Levi looked at Yasmin's furrowed brow. 'ONE MORE CHANCE!' he boomed in his best Ammi voice, before bursting out laughing.

Yasmin stared at the bald spot on the top of Mr Moustache's head as they sat either side of the checkers table. Mr Moustache had more hair on his top lip than he did on his head. Each time he bent down to make his next move, Yasmin caught sight of her own intense stare and screwed-up face reflected in the shiny circle on top of his head. This wasn't surprising. They were ten minutes into the game and Yasmin had already lost half of her pieces.

This had never happened before. Yasmin was worried.

Of course, she'd never had to play with a talking toy llama distracting her before. As soon as Yasmin reached a hand forward, Levi would yell, 'WAIT!' making her flinch and hesitate. Then he would offer useless advice like, 'Just take two turns in a row!' or 'Yell checkmate!' which would make Yasmin forget her move. She was starting to think that she might lose this match. Scanning the crowd, she noticed that Gilly was looking more worried than usual.

As Mr Moustache reached forward to make his next move, the front doorbell buzzed.

'I'll get the door. Pause the game!' yelled one OLD member, desperate for something to do. He shuffled to the door and opened it, but there was nobody there. 'Oh,' he said, rather deflated, and shuffled back to his seat.

But before Yasmin could even *think* about making her next move . . .

Buzz!

'I'll get it!' yelled another member before anyone else could volunteer. She slowly made her way up to the door and opened it but again, there was nobody there. 'Maybe someone's playing a prank on us,' she said.

'Goodie!' said one man, rubbing his hands together.

The doorbell started buzzing over and over again. *Buzz buzz buzzzzzzzz buzz buzzzz buzz!*

Then, in rapid succession with the buzzing, the lights in the leisure room started flicking on and off!

'Woohoo, it's a disco!' One man started waving

his hands in the air like he just didn't care. The other members of OLD started clapping the man along with his strange dancing – things were descending into chaos!

With a sinking feeling, Yasmin looked down at her bag. Sure enough, Levi was gone. She didn't know whether to jump up and seize him or wait for Levi to get bored. She was running out of time to make her next move. Not to mention the lights flicking on and off was making her eyes go funny.

'That's enough!' Mr Matthews, the OLD group leader, went over to the little box where the electric doorbell was fitted and pulled it straight off the wall. 'Now no one can interrupt the game.' He pulled open the electricity box by the front door and flipped the main switch back on, steadying the lights. Mr Matthews took his role as group leader *very seriously*.

A disappointed sigh went around the room. The OLD members had been enjoying their silent rave.

Yasmin took a deep breath and focused on the board.

Yes! She knew what to do.

She hopped back a space, but moved closer to one of Mr Moustache's key pieces. It was a clever trick. As long Mr Moustache didn't catch on, she could capture the piece.

A few moments passed. Mr Moustache was sitting with his head in his hand, staring down at the board intensely. He'd been sitting like that for a while now. Yasmin looked at the judge, who was timing the match.

'Player One! You must make your next move,' the judge barked at Mr Moustache.

Mr Moustache did not move.

'Player One! Your decision time is over!'

Mr Moustache suddenly let out an *almighty* **zzzzzzzzzZZZZZ.** He was *snoring*!

Gilly began cackling in her leather armchair, 'I think all that excitement was a bit much for him.'

'Or this place is so boring, he's fallen asleep!' Levi moaned, back behind the sofa. 'When can we get out of here?'

Even the sound of Gilly's laughter wasn't waking Mr Moustache up. He continued to snore, his little moustache twitching in the breeze from his nostrils.

'Maybe he's dreaming of winning the match!' Gilly howled, wiping the tears from her eyes.

The judge shrugged her shoulders. 'Well, Yasmin, since your opponent is unable to continue the game, you have won the match!'

The small group watching the game clapped wildly. Yasmin couldn't even bring herself to smile. She'd been so anxious about Levi messing things up that she'd spent the whole game super-stressed. She hadn't won the match through skill. It was just a forfeit! She felt close to tears as she was handed the winner badge.

'Yasmin, darling, what's wrong? That was the most fun we've had here in a while.' Gilly said, squeezing her in a hug.

Yasmin looked around at the other members of OLD – they were all smiling. Some were still even giggling about the doorbuzzer and the dancing. She widened her eyes in realisation. Levi had actually *helped* the residents.

Levi looked up at Yasmin's face. 'See? I know how to throw a good party.'

Yasmin just shook her head at Levi and squeezed Gilly back to reassure her. Then she quickly swooped up her bag. She wanted to get out of there before the residents thought she was being ungrateful or Levi played another trick.

As they walked through the doors, Levi craned his neck out of her backpack. 'Yas, I don't like how stressed out that checkers game makes you. You shoulda seen your face during the match. You looked like you had trapped wind.'

Just when Yasmin had started to feel a little bit grateful for Levi, he reminded her why he was a nuisance in the first place!

She got out her phone and tapped into the notes:

You were making me stressed, not checkers! And I don't need friends.

Levi squinted at the phone.

'Of course you need mates! Who are you gonna hang about with, play darts and watch footie, stuff like that?'

Yasmin walked briskly down the cobbled street on Brick Lane, staring straight ahead. She would have just ignored him, but now she was feeling defensive.

I hang out with myself. Or Gilly.

Levi huffed after reading the message. 'It's not the same. Look, this place ain't any good for you. I guess that Gilly's all right, but you need friends who are *kids.*'

Kids don't like me, Yasmin started to type, but then she deleted it. *Kids don't like hanging out with me*, she typed out instead. *I'm happy here playing the checkers matches.*

Levi shook his head as if he was a disappointed teacher. 'So does that mean we have to come back next week?'

Yasmin gave him a cautious nod.

'Hmm,' Levi turned his nose up in the air. 'We'll see about that.'

Yes, Yasmin thought with a fiery determination. They would see.

CHAPTER
FIFTEEN
Six Failures and
a Discovery

Now, I know you think that it sounds fun having a talking llama as a roommate. Especially one that loves breaking rules. But you would be wrong. Very wrong.

Yasmin spent most of the time running around after Levi, trying to guess his next move. The pesky llama was getting more confident now. More than once, she had seen him leaving the bathroom wrapped in a clean, white towel after a thirty-minute shower. She didn't know why he took so long, since he smelled just as bad as before and left little muddy footprints all over the bathtub, which Yasmin had to scrub clean.

She hadn't given up on getting rid of him. Oh no. That llama had caused enough trouble to last a lifetime, and Yasmin had had enough. She used her black sketch book to hatch plans to get rid of Levi, scribbling away first thing in the morning and late at night, rather like a mad scientist. And then she tried them all out.

Her first plan involves her dad's spade and the cover of nightfall.

But even being six feet under doesn't keep Levi down for long.

Yasmin takes advantage of 'pasta night' at home to execute her plan.

But Yasmin ends up getting in trouble for 'bringing' her toy to the dinner table.

In a moment of desperation Yasmin takes the towpath route to school and improvises with a shoelace.

Yet Yasmin should have known that Levi's contacts in the area would help him out of that scrape!

Yasmin quickly realised she would have to be smarter in her approach.

She felt a burning energy deep in her belly she had never experienced before. She was going to think of a plan so *foolproof* that Levi would never find his way back to her house again. And if she could find a way of doing that, then maybe the power would spread to other areas of her life . . .

She thought back to her birthday wish: *I wish I could stand up for myself.* She still didn't feel quite ready to do that with her parents, but she could definitely put in some practice on Levi.

One surprising upside of Levi's pranks was that Yasmin's brothers had eased off on their usual antics. In fact, they were now a bit wary of her after the bra incident, and so were finding ways of gently irritating without incurring her wrath. On the way to school each morning, they made sure to let her know just how strict their grandma, Daadi, was, with tales of her famous punishments. They had even offered to walk Yasmin *back* from school too, so that they could horrify her further.

'Once,' Tall Brother said as they trudged home, 'when Papa was small, he didn't wipe his sandals on the doormat, so Daadi wouldn't let him wear shoes for a month.'

'Last summer when Cousin Anwar went to see Daadi, she made him rub her feet as "entertainment" instead of watching TV. When he came home, he'd grown an extra finger on each hand.'

'Daadi used to have a cat, but she is soooooo boring, it pooed on her bed on purpose so that she would chuck it out.'

'A travelling salesman had tea at Daadi's house to sell her broadband and he DIED from BOREDOM!'

Yasmin had heard similar tales from relatives at family parties. Daadi was a no-nonsense lady who loved manners and rules more than her own husband (who had died years ago, though some said he'd run away in the night). According to Tall Brother, Daadi also hated checkers. This was a big surprise to Yasmin, who'd assumed that all elderly people enjoyed the game. It reminded Yasmin that she couldn't miss her tournament final. She wanted to win so badly, and she'd devoted so much time and practice to her gameplay.

Then, on Monday morning, Yasmin made a discovery.

She was creeping up the last set of stairs (after finding a rare five minutes when the bathroom was free) when she heard Levi's voice coming from inside her room. Who was he talking to? Another rat, or a pigeon perhaps? He'd better not have started inviting friends over, she thought.

Yasmin pressed her eye to the gap in the door and peered in. Levi was still underneath his laundry basket prison, but Yasmin's eyes bugged at the little silver flip phone in his foot. Where had he been hiding that?

'I know, Mama Llama,' Levi croaked into the phone.

Yasmin tried not to gasp in shock. Was Levi talking to his *mum*?

Levi coughed and rubbed his head with his free front leg. 'Yep. Thin ice, I know. And I am grateful you gave me another chance. She's a tough one to crack, wants to hang out with the olds. I keep telling her, it's kids all the way if you wanna have fun!'

A million questions raced through Yasmin's mind. One: it seemed like Levi wasn't alone in the world of talking toy llamas. Two: one of them was his mum. And three: she didn't seem too happy with him. If

Levi was in trouble with Mama Llama, could this be Yasmin's way out?

'I know, it's about the wish. But trust me, that's only gonna happen my way. I've got this. Okay, Mama Llama. Over and out.'

Levi tuck the little phone away in a location Yasmin couldn't quite see from behind the door. This was indeed interesting information. She needed to find out more before she could incorporate this into a new plan. Starting with finding that phone ...

She backed up a few paces and then, slightly louder than usual, marched into her room so Levi wouldn't know she'd been spying.

'Oh, quiet down, Stompy,' Levi moaned. 'I think I've got the flu.'

Yasmin hid a smirk. She did feel a *teeny weeny* bit guilty for leaving one of Auntie Gigi's snotty tissues next to Levi's bed, but none of her other plans had worked and she didn't want him coming to school again. It seemed to have done the trick – for now.

'I'm dyin', Yasmin,' Levi wailed overdramatically. 'And I never got to teach you . . .'

Yasmin cocked her head. Teach her what?

'Come . . . closer . . .' Levi whispered. 'I'm too weak to speak.'

Yasmin crept closer, for once actually interested in what the pest had to say.

'The real reason why I can speak, Yasmin, is – is – is – ACHHOOOOO!'

He sneezed fluff right in her face and started cackling away.

Yasmin immediately thumped her heaviest books down on top of the basket and chucked her duvet over the top.

'Fine by me love,' Levi shouted from within. 'I'm too ill to do anythin' anyway!'

Yasmin huffed. She should have known not to trust Levi by now. She just had to keep her fingers crossed that he would stay put. The final two matches that would qualify her for the checkers final were just around the corner. It was so close, she could taste it.

Warily, she glanced at his laundry basket.

She just had to get through the week. *Undisturbed.*

CHAPTER
SIXTEEN
Wormula
Bumbula

That week at school, Yasmin made sure to work extra hard in class, helping the other students with little notes and even tidying the desks during lunch break. She hoped that the teachers would report her good behaviour back to her parents. After all, who knew when Levi would strike next and she would be sent to Pakistan?

One thing was for sure. If Yasmin was going to Pakistan, then she was sending Levi on the next flight to Timbuktu.

Every day after school, as soon as she got through her door, she was greeted by a barrage of questions from Levi. On the odd occasion he'd been asleep, Yasmin had searched desperately under the basket and through her room, but hadn't found his secret

What happened at school?

phone anywhere. Then, as soon as Levi woke up, the questioning would start again. Yasmin had no idea why Levi cared so much about her life. Maybe he was just bored. But ever since that phone call to his mum, it seemed like he was interrogating her. It was the last thing she needed after a long day at school, and she usually just ignored him and put the TV on to shut him up. His favourite show was on channel 1090983 (a channel Yasmin never knew existed) and was called *I'm a Llama Get Me Out of Here!* Fifteen real llamas had been put in the jungle and had to do various challenges to win food for their camp. Mostly though,

Did you play with that fella again what's his name . . . Ezra! I told you it was all about the kids!

Why was Ammi shouting? I hope you gave it right back to her!

they stood

around and ate grass.

On Thursday night when one of the llama's would be sent home (e-llama-nation night), Levi had asked her another question.

'Why don't you wanna speak to me?'

Yasmin wrote him a question in return on her chalkboard. *Why can you speak?*

Levi looked down at his feet. 'Long story. Do you like me?'

Don't tell me those old bats are taking you shopping again!

Remember, you deserve to be heard Yasmin!

Yasmin was taken aback. Of course she didn't like him! He was making her life miserable. And yet . . . She looked at Levi perched on the end of her bed, munching on a chocolate digestive. It dawned on her that she had never done this before – watched TV in bed and eaten biscuits with someone. Even if that someone was a llama.

Maybe it was just because he was ill and looked so pitiful, but rather than shaking her head vigorously in answer to his question, Yasmin just rolled her eyes and handed him another biscuit.

Levi sighed. 'Well, I hope I hear yer voice one day.'

Yasmin smiled a little.

'I bet it sounds well weird . . . Trombone.' Levi looked at her. 'You won't go to them boring old fogeys again, will you?'

Yasmin chucked a pillow at him.

It was a long week, but Yasmin made it to Friday without any further tricks from the lurking llama, who had mostly been huddled up in bed with a cup of hot honey and lemon. At lunch break, Ezra had come to join her playing checkers once again and let her in on some news.

'I've got a surprise!' he said, leaning forward.

Yasmin cocked her head to one side.

'I'm coming to watch your game this afternoon!'

Yasmin frowned. What?

'The teachers said that playing checkers would help my concentration or something. So they told me to come with you to the oldie centre!' He drummed his hands on the table. 'Perfect, right?'

Yasmin inwardly panicked, her heart beating fast. OLD was HER special place, the only place she could just be herself. But with Ezra there, that would change. What if her elderly friends liked Ezra more than her . . . ? After all, he could play checkers *and* have a conversation with them. Plus, she'd never played checkers in front of someone from school before – especially not a potential friend. How was she supposed to concentrate with Ezra hovering over her shoulder?

Yasmin wrung her hands together and took a deep breath.

'Are you okay?' Ezra asked. 'My parents said I should ask you first before I come.'

Yasmin's panic subsided. That was nice of Ezra's parents. Her own parents would never think to ask her what she'd like. She got out a piece of paper and wrote a note.

Won't you get bored?

To her surprise, Ezra laughed. 'No! I like old people. They remind me of being with my grandpa.'

Yasmin looked at Ezra's smiling face. She supposed it couldn't hurt to let him come along. Some of the old ladies would nab him to play dominos or something as soon as they got in.

She mustered a smile and wrote another message.

OK.

It was a cheery, bright afternoon and Yasmin was trying to get into her game mindset. Having Ezra by her side was making it a bit more difficult, since he seemed interested in every single street sign, dog, kebab shop and sweet wrapper they passed.

Finally, after many pit stops, they were walking up the ramp to OLD and pushing the buzzer on the funky rainbow-coloured door. Mr Matthews, the group leader, answered. A look of concern spread across his wrinkled face.

'Oh, Yasmin, you're here!' he stuttered.

Yasmin nodded slowly. She always came on a Friday. Was Mr Matthews having what she heard Gilly call an 'elderly moment'?

'And you brought a friend!' Mr Matthews looked anxious. 'We thought that maybe you weren't coming this week, because of your . . . illness. That's what your letter said.'

Yasmin looked at Mr Matthews in confusion. What letter?

In the main sitting room, a group of OLD members were sitting in a circle. They were all huddled around a table, reading a piece of paper that Mrs Begum was holding.

'Yasmin, are you sure you should be out in public? You might still be infectious,' Mrs Begum said, a concerned look on her face.

Yasmin wrinkled her nose. Infectious? What was Mrs Begum talking about?

Mr Matthews lowered his voice. 'The worms,' he said seriously. 'In your posterior.'

'In her what?' Ezra asked.

'In her, um . . . . gluteus maximus,' Mr Matthews mumbled.

Yasmin opened her mouth wide in shock.

'Oh!' Ezra piped up. 'You mean her bum!'

'Yes. Bum worms,' one of the old ladies shouted

across the room.

'*Wormula bumbula*, I think is the medical term,' said Mr Matthews with a knowing look. 'I'm sorry, Yasmin, but as OLD leader I have to put the group first. We had a bad case of bum worms last year. We can't risk another outbreak'

'I couldn't bring myself to eat spaghetti for weeks,' a greying man added. 'It was a dark time for all of us.'

All the OLD people shook their heads sadly, remembering the Great Bum Worm Plague of 2019.

'For goodness sake!' said Gilly, raising her voice over the concerned murmurs. 'Would you all stop saying bum worms?' She turned to Yasmin. 'Darling, are you feeling poorly?'

Yasmin shook her head vigorously, bright red with embarrassment.

'There, see?' Gilly told the crowd. 'I think this might be someone's idea of a naughty prank. Perhaps one of the other children from school, Yasmin?'

Yasmin was mortified. This was worse than the Purple/Poo Incident! And now she was thinking about *that* as well, which was making her MORE embarrassed. She couldn't even bring herself to look at Ezra, who was most definitely thinking about bum worms and whether she had them.

With her cheeks burning red she made a run for the upstairs toilets. How could she play checkers in front of all these people now? And who had written a letter about her having bum worms?

A single thought stopped her in her tracks as she was halfway up the stairs.

Who had said he didn't want her to go to OLD again?

She was going to kill that llama!!

'Yasmin –' Ezra said quietly. He had followed her up the staircase. 'Please don't be embarrassed.'

Yasmin did her best to collect herself and bravely turned around.

'You've been practising every lunchtime. It would be a shame to give up now. Don't you want to go through to the semi-finals?'

Yasmin was surprised that Ezra had noticed her practising. She bit her lip and peeped over at the living room, where all the OLD members were still whispering amongst themselves.

'Don't bother about them,' Ezra said, shaking his head. 'I've seen better behaved two-year-olds. Plus, did you hear how many times they said bum?'

This made Yasmin smirk a little.

'And if it makes you feel better,' Ezra whispered, 'I've had bum worms twice.'

Yasmin burst out laughing.

'Glad I could help,' Ezra said.

He led her back down the staircase where a group of ladies were waiting.

'Young man!' One of the ladies smiled at Ezra. 'Would you like to come and have a biscuit with us? We can play dominoes.'

Yasmin's stomach sank. After his pep talk, she really wanted Ezra there when she was playing. But no doubt he'd get distracted, and go off and play with someone new.

'No thanks,' Ezra chirped. 'I'm going to watch my friend play checkers.'

Yasmin froze. There was that word again. *Friend.*

Gilly pushed through the group of ladies and grabbed Yasmin and Ezra before they could be poached by another bored OLD member.

'Let's get to business. Welcome to OLD,' Gilly said to Ezra. 'Yasmin? I believe you have a checkers game to play.'

Yasmin nodded. She did.

And a case of imaginary bum worms wasn't going to hold her back.

CHAPTER SEVENTEEN
A Fish for School

Yasmin spent yet another checkers match in a state of intense worry, convinced Levi would pop up and turn everything upside down. That bum worms letter had *almost* had her chucked out of the competition. It was only by extreme concentration (and Ezra's encouragement) that she managed to win. The next match she played would be the semi-finals of the whole competition!

This couldn't go on. Levi was a threat to her family life, her checkers trophy and now, a potential friend. Ezra was okay about the whole bum worm thing (thank goodness!) but she couldn't risk Levi embarrassing her any further. She didn't want to lose another friend for being 'weird'.

Levi had to go.

First thing on Monday morning, Yasmin headed out of the house with Ammi. In her rucksack was a strange package wrapped in a plastic bag. This time, she wasn't taking any chances. She had blindfolded Levi with one of her old socks so that he wouldn't be able to memorise the way back to her house. She had been careful not to cover his mouth. After all, he still needed to breathe. Or did he? Did toy llamas breathe? Anyway, she didn't want to be a llama-killer, so she left his mouth free.

Levi yelped, 'OW OW OW OW OW OW OW OW...' all the way down the road. Yasmin clenched her jaw. Soon, they would be on the corner of Brushfield Street, where she had convinced Ammi to take a detour on the way to school.

They were starting a new science project at school. Each student had to choose what topic they wanted to study. Originally, Yasmin had chosen the Bengal tiger. Then Papa had decided on moss growth. Now Yasmin needed a reason for Ammi to take her back to the market, and in a panic that morning she had only come up with one idea.

'ISTILLDON'TUNDERSTANDWHYYOUNEED FISHFORSCHOOL,' Ammi yelled.

Yasmin had written Ammi a note saying that she had chosen to study tuna instead of moss. Meaning she had to bring a whole tuna fish to school.

'BUTYOUWOULDN'TBRINGABENGALTIGER?' Ammi questioned.

They both regarded each other for a moment.

'WILLITHELPYOUGETBETTERMARKS?'

Yasmin smiled eagerly.

Ammi nodded. 'FINE.'

Yasmin gave her a big hug in relief. Ammi patted her on the back. 'LET'SGO.'

The market was bustling with traders who were setting up for the day. They hurried about, pulling large white sheets over their tables and wiping down the displays. The sun had already risen and they were keen to begin trade.

Ammi spotted the fishmonger unloading his tuna on to the trays full of ice on his stall. As she hurried up to him and began bartering for a good deal, Yasmin quickly slipped over to the bric-a-brac stalls.

She spied the man who had sold Levi bending over his car boot, his bottom wiggling behind him. Quickly, she looked around. Her eyes passed over dolls with matted hair, various trinket boxes in different sizes and countless rows of old dusty books. Where was the bargain bucket? She finally peered over the display table and saw it on the other side, hiding behind a large chest of old ladies' nighties.

Keeping an eye on the man to make sure he still had his back turned, Yasmin crawled underneath the display table and crept over to the bucket. Then she pulled Levi from her bag and shoved him deep inside.

'Oof, where am I? It smells like cheesy crisps in here,' he grumbled.

Yasmin was kind enough to remove the plastic bag, but kept the sock firmly over his eyes. Then she pulled out a label she had made and tied it around Levi's neck. It said: FREE TO A GOOD HOME! in bold red letters.

'Don't you get it yet?' Levi whined. 'I'm just gonna keep coming back! You *need* me!'

Yasmin fully intended this to be the last time she ever saw Levi, but she supposed he could have one more chance to explain himself. She got out her phone and wrote in the notes: *Why?* Then she held the phone up close to Levi's face, since he didn't have his reading glasses on and his eyesight was terrible.

'You need me because . . .' Levi scrunched up his plastic nose. 'Well . . . because I can help you make younger mates, and stand up for yourself, and – and . . . we can hang out.'

I don't want to hang out with you!

'But . . . who will I hang out with then?' Levi said,

slipping down into the bargain bucket.

That sounds like YOU need ME. Not the other way round.

Yasmin held the phone up to Levi's nose one last time, and then quickly popped it back in her pocket. The llama hadn't given her any good reason to keep him around. In fact, he'd done the opposite.

She heaped the other toys on top of Levi, making sure he was securely hidden. She had to hurry as Ammi would be wondering where she was. She took one last look at the bargain bucket. Even if Levi did manage to escape, he wouldn't know the way back to Yasmin. Then some other child might see him wandering about with the sign around his neck and take him home. He could cause havoc there instead.

'MYDAUGHTERNEEDSATUNA.' Ammi was making conversation with the fishmonger as he wrapped the tuna for her. 'DON'TASKMEWHY.'

Yasmin scuttled over. The fishmonger slowly handed the large, heavy fish to her with a puzzled expression. Yasmin took the moist bundle in both arms and headed for the exit.

'THANKS,' Ammi shouted and followed Yasmin out.

'You're welcome?' the fishmonger called after them.

Yasmin breathed a sigh of relief. She may have to carry a whole tuna around at school, but at least she'd got rid of Levi.

MISSION ACCOMPLISHED!

CHAPTER EIGHTEEN
Something Fishy's Going On . . .

Yasmin and her smelly tuna were sitting in history class, listening to Miss Zainab. Yasmin was finding it much easier to concentrate without the threat of Levi turning up, and was enjoying Miss Zainab's lesson on her favourite thing: ancient civilisations.

They'd moved on to the Incas, and the promise of human sacrifice had even captured Ezra's imagination. He sat dutifully next to Yasmin, chewing on his pencil and doodling a gruesome sheep with crosses for eyes.

'The Incas worshipped many gods for different occasions,' Miss Zainab said, gesturing to the board. 'For example, Pacha Mama, who was the goddess of the earth, and Urcuchillay, the god of animals who shepherds prayed to, to protect their livestock.'

'What about the sacrifices?' Ezra blurted, only remembering to put his hand up after asking the question.

'Well, Ezra, since you did put your hand up eventually . . .' Miss Zainab said with a twinkle. 'Sacrifices, human or animal, happened on important occasions, like the beginning of a new moon cycle. Of course, this all happened a very long time ago. We don't sacrifice humans any more, thank goodness!'

Yasmin was about to write a question for her teacher about the Incan gods when Miss Zainab paused by her desk, wrinkling her nose. 'Uh, Yasmin? What's that fishy smell?'

Yasmin pointed to her bag.

'Is that your lunch?' Miss Zainab asked.

Yasmin paused, then nodded. She didn't want Miss Zainab telling her science teacher to expect a fish in class. She needed to get rid of it before anyone passed out from the smell.

'Maybe you should go give it to the lunch lady to put in the fridge.' Miss Zainab pinched her nose with her fingers. 'Hurry along!'

Yasmin obediently left the classroom and headed for the playground, where there were two large dustbins. She snuck down the corridor to the double doors. Peering out, she checked that the coast was clear. She was reliving her short time as a secret agent, but this time she was going to do it right.

The playground was empty so she hurried out, removing the smelly package and flopping the fish into the bin. It hit the bottom of the metal container with a moist *SPLAT*.

'Lunch! I love sushi!'

Yasmin screamed and then clamped her mouth shut. She couldn't be seen out here! Or heard – wait, had she just screamed?

Levi popped his head out of the top of the bin. 'Yassy, you made a noise!' He clapped, then added seriously, 'There's something I have to tell you.'

Hastily, Yasmin chucked a bin bag on top of Levi. He wriggled his way out.

'Honestly Yasmin, we got to talk,' he said. 'I know I've upset you.'

Yasmin quickly slammed the bin lid shut and ran back inside. Her heart was pounding. Would she ever get rid of him? Is this what the rest of her life would be like? How had he even got back here?

I can answer that one. And I'll do it, dear reader, in a limerick:

There once was a Levi the Llama,
Whose owner thought he caused too much drama
She put him in a bin,
So he hired a pigeon
To fly him to school and alarm-her.

. . . Thank you, thank you very much.

Yasmin rushed back to the classroom, her mind racing with even more frantic questions: Why did

Levi keep showing up at the most inconvenient times? When was the last time she had screamed? Had her scream sounded normal?

She rushed back into class and sat down at her desk, pretending to be incredibly interested in a doodle scratched into the table. A bead of sweat dripped from her forehead on to her paper.

Ezra nudged her and mouthed, 'Are you okay?'

Wiping the sweat away, Yasmin nodded vigorously and tried to avoid eye contact.

'Yasmin, we have moved on to ten minutes of silent reading now,' Miss Zainab called from her desk.

Yasmin loved reading. Perhaps enough to get completely lost in a book and forget that she was being stalked by a stuffed toy with zero social skills and poor eyesight. She looked in her rucksack with trembling hands. Someone had replaced her reading book with the *Llamas of London* magazine. So much for forgetting about Levi. Nevertheless, she got it out, opening the page to a description of 'The Hackney Llama Mandem'. She began reading, her eyes darting across the page.

The Hackney Llama Mandem are a group of five urban toy llamas living in –

'Ppssshhht!' A little voice came from below the desk.

– living in Clapton. The leader is Reginald Jones, a black-haired toy llama who came over from Jamaica in 1974 –

'Ppppsssssssssssshhhhhhhhhhhht!' The voice came again.

– Reginald came alone. As we know, a llama is nothing without his herd, being very sociable creatures. So, he was tasked with forming the Hackney Llama Mandem in 1985 –

'PSHT! YASMIN!'

The magazine slipped from her sweaty, shaky hands. Miss Zainab looked up from her desk and Yasmin gave her an apologetic smile. She finally looked down.

'We neeeeed to chat,' said Levi.

Yasmin kicked him away in desperation. If llamas were sociable creatures, then why was Levi on his own? Why wasn't he with his flipping herd? There were just ten minutes to go until breaktime. She turned the page of *Llamas of London*.

- Reginald was sent to Clapton on official SNH business, tasked with delivering an important -

'Arrgghh!'

The class looked up in shock. It wasn't Tia shrieking over a rubber this time.

It was Miss Zainab.

The teacher had just opened her desk drawer to get out her red marking pen when . . .

SPLAT!

A tuna head had flown out of the drawer and slapped her in the face.

Everyone in the room gasped. Everyone but Ezra, who held his breath until it looked like he might explode. And then –

'HAHAHAHAHHAAHHAHAHAHAHAHAHAHA-HAHAHHAAH!'

'YASMIN SHAH and EZRA ISAAC!' Miss Zainab boomed, fish slime dripping off her chin. Ezra slapped the desk and howled, his whole body shaking. 'Go straight to the headteacher's office. NOW!'

Levi was back under Yasmin's desk.

'Well,' he said, almost guiltily as Yasmin stared at him in complete horror. 'You were ignoring me.'

CHAPTER NINETEEN
Levi Spills the Beans

In all the years that Yasmin Shah had attended Fish Lane Primary School, she had not once been given detention. Yet, here she was for the second time in two weeks, sitting in silence and watching the clock tick by slowly.

Levi had tried to convince her that it was 'character-building' to get detention. Yasmin wasn't convinced. She stared blankly at the empty whiteboard, and thought about everything that had led her to this point.

Had she made the right decisions? Should she have tried harder to stand up for herself? She was uncertain. The only thing she was absolutely sure of was that Levi was to blame. Ever since that awful day when he came tumbling out of the cupboard, her life had gone from bad to worse. Whatever had caused Levi to come to life, whether magic or mutation, was a curse.

Each second seemed to pass slower in the detention room. Even the headteacher, who always supervised after-school detention, was nodding off, her head drooping over the marking on her desk. There were only three students to watch over: Yasmin, a small boy called Owen and Ezra.

Ezra was trying to concentrate on his homework. He tapped his pencil repeatedly against the desk, drumming a little rhythm with his eyes closed. Levi joined in, clicking his heels on the hard floor in time with Ezra's drumming. Yasmin put her fingers in her ears, but she could still hear the *tap, tap, tap* of the llama's feet. It was like someone had given tap shoes to a colony of ants.

Ezra smiled at Yasmin, giving her a thumbs up. Yasmin gave him a quick mournful wave in reply. She aimed another firm kick towards Levi, who went scampering out of the room.

'Excuse me Miss,' Owen piped up. 'My pen exploded!'

The headteacher blinked awake. 'That's the second time today, Owen! You must stop chewing it.' She sighed and gestured to the door. 'Ezra, can you take Owen to the boys' toilets to wash out his mouth? And then go to lost property and get him a clean shirt.'

The two boys trooped out of the classroom, with Ezra trying to stifle a giggle at the blue ink spilling down Owen's chin like a strange beard.

Almost as soon as the boys were out in the corridor, the school receptionist popped his head round the door with a worried look on his face.

'Very sorry to bother you,' he said, 'but there is a small issue with the staff-room fish tank.'

'What sort of issue?' the headteacher snapped.

The receptionist glanced over at Yasmin and lowered his voice. 'Somebody appears to have tried to feed the fish with, uh, chocolate digestives.'

'Whatever next?' the headteacher sighed, getting up from the desk. 'I'll be right there. Wait here please, Yasmin.'

Chocolate digestives? Something seemed fishy to Yasmin, and it wasn't the actual fish.

A few moments later, Levi came trotting back into the classroom, a little out of breath.

'Finally!' he exhaled, jumping up on the desk. 'I thought I'd never get you alone.'

Yasmin threw her hands in the air. That was it! She wasn't going to take any more of Levi and his mission to ruin her life! She grabbed a piece of paper and wrote in angry letters:

LEAVE ME ALONE!!!

'But that's just it, Yasmin,' Levi replied. 'I can't.'

WHY???

Yasmin scratched into the paper so hard that it tore through. Writing wasn't enough to express how angry she was.

WHY?

WHY?

WHY?

*WHYYYYYYYYYYYYYYYYYYYYYYYYYYYYYYYYY
YYYYYYYYY!!!!!!????????????*

'Because I'M YOUR GUARDIAN LLAMA!' Levi
shouted.

Yasmin fell off her chair.

'See, *that's* what I was trying to avoid,' Levi
remarked.

He jumped off the desk and tugged on Yasmin's
sleeve with his mouth to help her up. She settled
back in her chair, shaking her head. *A guardian
llama?* This was definitely the most ridiculous thing
Levi had ever said.

She grabbed her pen and wrote in capitals:

TELL ME EVERYTHING

Levi scratched behind his ear. 'I've already told
you a bit too much –'

Yasmin jabbed her finger at the page again.

EVERYTHING

Levi sighed. 'Obviously this all happened well before my time, but there was this guy. He was like a god of animals. He lived in Ancient Peru and his name was Ur . . . Urcul-something.'

URCUCHILLAY, Yasmin wrote. She knew she'd been paying extra attention in that history class for a reason.

'How'd you know that?' Levi seemed impressed. 'Anyway, he was sick of us llamas being sacrificed all

the time at the beginning of every moon cycle. He was a llama himself, you see – multicoloured, so sick! So he used his magic to cast a spell. Instead of thirty llamas being sacrificed at the beginning of the month, he saved them by turning them into toy llamas. The spell continues to this day. That's how I was made. I used to be a real llama, and then one day – *pop*! Here I was in the fluff. It's way better being a magic toy than a real llama, let me tell you. I can travel the world!'

Yasmin stared at Levi, unblinking, for a good minute in silence. Then she wrote:

So you ARE actually magic?

Levi cocked an eyebrow. 'I'm a talking toy llama, Yasmin. Of course I'm magic! It's well better than standing around eating grass.'

And there are other toy llamas . . . like you?

'I'm not really meant to tell you this bit either,' said Levi. 'But since those early days, we've become more organised. As toys, we can do anything and go anywhere without raising eyebrows. Llamas love kids, so we tasked ourselves with being guardians for children across the world! There's a whole network of us. We're called the *Seen Not Herd* group. I'm surprised you didn't figure it out from *Llamas of London*.'

Yasmin remembered the section about Reginald following official orders from SNH . . . **S**een **N**ot **H**erd!

'We can be seen by anyone as normal toy llamas, but not heard,' Levi explained. 'Each llama is assigned a kid to help, plus we *love* hanging out with kids. That's why I'm here. To help you!'

Yasmin grabbed her pen again. She had so many questions (especially about the multicoloured llama god) but the main thing she wanted to say was:

You haven't helped. AT ALL!

'My methods are a bit . . . unconventional,' Levi admitted. 'I ain't done this for a while. The head agent of the Seen Not Herd group is Mama Llama.

She assigned me to you to see if I've still got it. If I don't help you, Mama Llama says I'll be turned into a stupid farm animal again and I'll have to stay in a rubbish paddock all day with no friends.'

So *that* was who Levi had been chatting to on the phone. Mama Llama wasn't his mum. She was his boss!

I don't need your help!!!!!! Yasmin wrote, scribbling at the page with tears in her eyes.

'Yes you do!' Levi insisted. 'You made a wish on your birthday – to be able to stand up for yourself. I'm here to make that come true, and to help you hang out with more youngsters. I thought if I just annoyed you enough, eventually you'd speak up. It ain't *quite* worked out the way I wanted,' he admitted.

Yasmin tore up the paper and threw the pieces into the air. She let herself cry all the tears she'd been trying to hold back. How did this menace think he was helping? Why did this have to happen to *her?* WHAT ON EARTH WAS A MAMA LLAMA?

'Oh, love, don't cry.' Levi's tail hung between his legs. 'I – I... I'm sorry, all right?' He seemed surprised at the words that had come out of his mouth.

At that moment, Ezra came sloping into the classroom. He was alone.

'I'm back!' he sang, before stopping short at the sight of Yasmin in tears. 'What happened?'

Yasmin shook her head and turned away.

Ezra sat down at the desk next to Yasmin. He started picking up the little pieces of torn-up paper and arranging them on the desk. 'It's okay, I don't like people seeing me cry either,' he said, sliding the pieces of paper around. 'But sometimes, when I tell my mum what's making me sad, I don't feel sad any more. It's weird.'

Yasmin sniffed and wiped her eyes. Even if she preferred to be alone, Ezra was trying to be nice. And after being harassed by a llama all day, she appreciated niceness.

'If you don't tell anyone what's making you sad, then they won't be able to fix it,' Ezra went on. 'Like when a little engine light flashes behind the car steering wheel. It's telling you there's something wrong with the engine.'

He finished pushing around the pieces of paper on the desk. He'd formed them into a smiley face.

Yasmin considered his words. They seemed to make sense, although nothing in her life was making sense at the moment. It was all one confusing llama-shaped disaster. Plus she'd just had a whole lesson on Ancient Peru that would definitely not be coming up in history class.

She got out a new piece of paper and wrote:

Thank you.

Ezra smiled, 'No problem. That's what friends are for, right?'

Yasmin nodded slowly. That's what friends were for.

The headteacher popped her head around the

door, tapping her watch. 'It's half four now, you're free to go. Oh and don't do it again. Detention is boring for *everyone*, including the teachers.'

4.30pm!? Yasmin's head shot around to look at the clock. She was going to be late for her checkers semi-final at OLD! All the talk of llama gods and magical toys had completely taken her mind off the competition.

Hurriedly she began packing away her things.

'What's the rush?' Ezra asked, watching Yasmin zip up her bag.

Yasmin wrote the letters *OLD* in the air with her finger.

Ezra's eyes widened in understanding. 'The semi-final! Can I come? My mum doesn't get home from work until 5.30.'

Yasmin nodded and gestured frantically for him to follow. Any later, and she might miss her slot!

She didn't know that something *much* worse than that was about to happen.

CHAPTER TWENTY
Chaos, Thy Name is Llama

Yasmin's opponent for the semi-final match was a ninety-two-year-old gentleman named Dennis Wrinklebottom. He was nicknamed Dennis the Menace, not because of his striped top, but because he had a tendency to chase pigeons down Brick Lane on his mobility scooter. There had been six such accidents since he'd got his licence back in March.

If you're thinking that you don't need a licence to ride a mobility scooter, you're correct. The local council invented scooter licences specifically for Dennis the Menace Wrinklebottom. Please, reader, look both ways before crossing the street. I would hate for you to face the same fate as those pigeons, RIP.

As obvious as it might seem, nobody ever made fun of Dennis's last name. Mr Wrinklebottom had put up with it for his entire life. By now, he had heard every single joke in the book. Anyway, how much funnier could you make a name like Wrinklebottom? If you can think of a way, please do send me a letter.

With all the fuss and drama of zooming through the door *just in time* for her match, all eyes were now on Yasmin as she took her seat at the checkers table. If there were two things OLD loved, they were fuss and drama. Of course, Ezra was also watching. It was actually quite nice having a team mate to cheer her on, even if that team mate did periodically wander off to play with some shiny object he'd seen across the room.

The stopwatch started and the game began.

The tension built. It was touch and go for a while with Dennis and Yasmin level-pegging.

Then, within three moves, Yasmin captured four of Dennis's pieces and was heading towards gaining a king. Ezra was standing close to Gilly who had given him a 'Go Yasmin' banner she'd made. Each time Yasmin captured a piece Ezra nodded his head, enraptured, and held the banner up.

Dennis's shaky hands hopped one of his black pieces over Yasmin's white piece, capturing it for himself.

Suddenly, Yasmin noticed something out of the corner of her eye. A furry leg, protruding from a bookcase in the corner of the room. It was holding

a small sign. A sign that said, 'Go Dennis!'

Yasmin banged her fist on the table, making Dennis yelp. Some guardian llama Levi was! Even if he thought he was 'helping' by stopping her hanging out here, she wasn't about to let him sabotage her game.

She deliberately sacrificed her piece to move to the end of the board. Now she had a king piece, and could move backwards to secure the rest of Dennis's pieces. Gilly clapped her hands.

'You've got this, Yasmin!' Ezra whispered excitedly.

Yasmin smiled at him. It was the sixth minute, and very clear that she was in the lead. Dennis was falling straight into her trap, moving around the board where she secretly led him. He furrowed his big bushy eyebrows and muttered to himself a few times before looking up at his opponent. A menace on the streets does not make you a menace on the checkers board.

'Well Yasmin,' he sighed, offering Yasmin a big pat on the back and a raisin cookie. 'You've beaten me!'

Yasmin beamed. She was going to the checkers tournament finals, with no chaos involved!

But chaos was Levi the llama's middle name.

Levi Chaos the Llama.

(It had sounded better in his head.)

CHAPTER TWENTY-ONE
The Golden (OLDie) Rules

'Phhst! Yasmin!' Levi hissed from behind a teapot.

'What I'm about to do is for your own good!'

Yasmin's tummy lurched. This couldn't be good.

Luckily, Levi kept his llama landline close by at all times.

Now to wait for the perfect time to hit 'send'.

Yasmin located Levi under the tea trolley and kicked it sharply. The cups rattled noisily.

'Are you all right, Yasmin?' Gilly asked at the unexpected outburst.

Yasmin tried to smile reassuringly, although she ended up just looking rather constipated.

'She's probably just excited to have won,' Ezra assured Gilly.

Yasmin nodded and tried to keep her eyes away from the tea trolley.

'You're not gonna learn to stand up for yourself here,' Levi continued. 'You need friends your own age. Trust me. I've got this.'

A *whooshing* sound came from his phone. He'd sent the email.

Oh no.

Yasmin flung her hand underneath the tea trolley and snatched the mobile from Levi's grasp.

Too late.

Mr Matthew's phone pinged. He jumped. 'I'm still

not used to this thing, scares the living daylights out of me,' he grumbled. Perching his reading glasses on the end of his nose, he peered at the phone.

'What is it, Matthew?' Gilly asked.

Yasmin was too anxious to even wonder what had possessed his parents to call their son Matthew Matthews.

'Well,' he said, squinting at his phone. 'It seems to be an email from a concerned OLD member. A *Mr L. Ama.*'

'I don't remember him,' Gilly mused.

That fleabag! thought Yasmin. *And what a stupid name!* He could at least have tried Sir Llamalot, or Dr Haymuncher.

Mr Matthews cleared his throat.

'Dear Mr Leader of the OLD place,' he read. 'It has come to my attention during a routine visit to your group that you have someone participating in the black and white circle game thingy that SHOULD NOT be playing. In fact, she should not be allowed on these premises AT ALL!'

The whole room of OLD members collectively gasped. *Drama.*

'What on earth is he talking about?' Gilly said.

Suddenly, the OLD handbook came sliding out from underneath the tea trolley at an alarming speed. It came to an abrupt stop as it bashed against Mr Matthews' ankles, and fell open on the page that had been earmarked and stamped especially for this moment.

Tentatively, Mr Matthews picked it up. He read out Rule Number One. 'Members must not be any younger than eighty years old.'

'Then why is Yasmin allowed to come every week?' Mrs Begum pondered.

'Because of her school programme, remember?' Gilly said, rising from her armchair.

Yasmin knew that things were bad then. Gilly only stood up in extreme emergencies. Once when the toaster had caught fire and everyone evacuated,

Gilly refused to move until the firefighters carried her out.

'But she *is* only nine years old,' Mr Matthews countered.

Yasmin held up ten fingers.

'Okay ten years old. That's still seventy years off,' Mr Matthews said.

'Yasmin is a special case,' Gilly said, stepping in front of Yasmin.

This was *really bad,* Mr Matthews did not like being challenged.

'But Mr Patel isn't? Even though he's eighty in one week's time?'

An excited group of OLD members clustered around, watching the back and forth like a tennis match.

Gilly looked flustered. 'Yasmin has always come on a Friday!'

'Rules are rules, Miss Gillian. As OLD group leader I *have* to uphold the rules.' Mr Matthews plonked the handbook right on top of the checkers board, sending checkers pieces flying everywhere. Some even landed in the cups of tea on the trolley.

'What's so special about those stupid rules anyway?' Ezra demanded. 'Yasmin is eighty at heart!' He paused. 'Wait, that came out wrong.'

'Are you *absolutely sure*, Matthew?' Gilly pleaded. 'Isn't there *anything* in there about special exceptions?'

Mr Matthews studied the handbook once more.

He read Rule Number One.

He read Rule Number Two.

Then he read Rule Number One again.

And then he read Rule Number Two again, just to be sure.

Yasmin gulped. Her fate lay in Mr Matthews' hands.

He scratched his head. 'It says that members have to be of a certain *mature* age . . .'

Gilly quickly interjected, 'But Yasmin *is* a very

mature ten-year-old.'

At that moment, the tea trolley next to Yasmin flipped over, sending tea and digestives flying everywhere.

'Surprise!' Levi shouted at Yasmin as he jumped out of the trolley with a biscuit in his mouth.

'Oohhh!' squealed an elderly lady, clapping her hands together in delight.

The llama had already dashed back into Yasmin's bag. She looked frantically around her but, of course, no one else could hear or see Levi. All they could see was Yasmin and thirty pounds' worth of good quality digestives splattered across the floor.

'Does THAT seem mature to you, Miss Gillian?' Mr Matthews said.

'You upset her,' Ezra said in Yasmin's defence. 'It's not her fault she got angry!'

Yasmin grabbed Ezra's arm and tried to get him to stop talking. But Gilly and Ezra were doing the arguing for her.

'Matthew, she has the checkers tournament to win, you can't chuck her out now!' Gilly was turning very pink in the cheeks.

Mr Matthews marched to the funky door and flung it open. 'Yasmin, the email from Mr L. Ama is correct,' he said, trying to look as stern as possible. 'Our members' handbook clearly states all members need to be *at least* eighty years old or – or, *no younger* than eighty or – oh, whatever! Mr Patel will be able to join next week, and we need to make

room for him. I'm sorry.'

'Well, then I'm leaving too!' Gilly exclaimed.

She picked up her coat, ready to march out. Yasmin stopped her. Levi had already spoiled Yasmin's chance of winning the championship. Gilly didn't deserve to lose out on her special club as well.

'Are you sure Yasmin?' Gilly asked.

Yasmin nodded, her nose snotty from crying. It was the most difficult decision she had ever made,

but she knew she would have to leave OLD. Once word got back to Fish Lane Primary School about Yasmin's 'biscuit-throwing tantrum', they would never let her go back as the School Representative anyway.

Gilly wiped the tears from Yasmin's cheeks and then turned sharply back to Mr Matthews. 'I believe it is *your* turn to clear the tea trolley this week, Matthew.'

With a deep sigh, Yasmin picked up her bag and left OLD and checkers behind.

'Yasmin, wait!'

Ezra tried to follow her. Yasmin stormed on ahead, too ashamed to face him.

'Free from them old fogies at last!' Levi cheered from inside her bag. 'Now you can hang out with some proper mates your own age. Kids are the *best*.'

Yasmin zipped her bag shut tightly.

She'd lost the one thing she cared about the most.

CHAPTER TWENTY-TWO
The Importance of Friends

Yasmin plonked Levi on her bed. He looked at her red and puffy eyes.

'I know you're sad now, but you're better off in the long run,' he said. 'Trust me! I am your guardian llama, after all.'

Yasmin's technique of ignoring Levi wasn't working. He was just too loud. So she decided to do something she had never done before. She decided to confront the problem head on.

She wrote in big letters on the chalk board behind her bed:

I was happy at OLD.

Levi seemed confused. 'But they were so . . . ANCIENT. Kids is where it's at, Yasmin. Kids!'

They were my friends.

Yasmin's chalk was almost running out with all the writing she was doing. But she needed to get through to Levi.

Levi squinted at Yasmin's message. 'Being a real llama is rubbish,' he said unexpectedly. 'You just stand around all day munching hay. There's no kids to play with. What's the point?'

BOOHOO! Yasmin angrily wrote on the board. Levi had taken away the only thing she loved and now she was supposed to feel sorry for *him?*

She picked up one of her books – *The Importance of Friends* – and threw it at Levi. He peered at the writing.

'I don't have me glasses on,' he moaned.

Yasmin picked him up roughly and held his head next to the front cover.

'F-R-I-E-N-D-S,' Levi read slowly. 'Oh, mates! Yeah, that's right! We're mates! You and me, Yassy! Young and cool, that's us!'

Mates?! Yasmin scrawled in disbelief.

'Oh . . . I see how it is.' Levi walked grumpily over to the pillow and snuggled himself down inside, smearing his dirty feet on the white linen.

They both sat in silence for a moment. Well, Yasmin was always silent. But now she sat very still as well.

It was all over. Her checkers tournament, her time at OLD. If Levi was only going to leave once he'd 'helped' her find mates and stand up for herself, then there was no way she'd get rid of him. She would never learn to stand up for herself, or make real friends with Ezra, or even keep the friends she had at OLD. Levi had ruined her life.

She picked Levi up and put him underneath his laundry-basket prison. Then she turned off the light and headed out to the stairs to use the bathroom. Behind her, she heard Levi murmur: 'I was just trying to help.'

She ignored him and padded down the stairs, patting her pocket where she felt a rectangle shape. Levi's phone.

It was time to call Mama Llama.

CHAPTER TWENTY-THREE
Yasmin calls the Shots

Under the flickering electric light of the bathroom, Yasmin unlocked Levi's llama landline. She clicked on to the contacts page and started scrolling down the list.

A-ha.

She clicked. Some
details came up, along
with a thumbnail
picture. In it, a sandy-
haired toy llama with a
pair of snazzy red spectacles
smiled with big teeth at the
camera.

Mama Llama.

Yasmin knew that Levi was in trouble with Mama
Llama already. If she complained, then who knew
what might happen to him?

But then it hit her. The thought that she would
never go to OLD again. The only place where she
had peace – the only place she fitted in. She screwed
up her fists in anger. Levi didn't want to help her.
He just didn't want to get turned back into a real
llama! For half the year she had been working up to
winning the checkers trophy, practising at every

spare moment and defeating a whole string of difficult opponents. All for nothing.

And it was Levi's fault.

Yasmin turned her attention back to the phone with a scowl. She couldn't call Mama Llama for obvious reasons. Although it didn't seem formal enough, she'd have to send a text.

Dear Mama Llama,

You need to know that the guardian llama you sent me has RUINED MY LIFE. I don't know what type of company you run but it ISN'T WORKING. He is a massive pain in the bum and has done nothing but cause problems. Please. Sort. It. Out.

From Yasmin (angry child)

As she wrote, the anger she felt got greater and greater until she practically smashed the 'Send' button.

Whoosh.

A little tick came up next to her message. *Sent.*

Yasmin stood for a while, panting with the effort of sending such a furious message.

It was what he deserved, she told herself. And she kept repeating that, all the way back up the several flights of stairs to her room, where she paused. She could hear Levi snoring inside. Typical. Another night's sleep, ruined.

Yasmin crept into her room and slid Levi's llama landline back under the laundry basket. As she got changed for bed, she realised just how heavy she felt, like she was carrying huge stones in her pockets. Her feet ached and her head was thumping. It had been a long, sad day. Without OLD and checkers and Ezra to look forward to, maybe every day would feel like this.

She slid into bed and turned to face away from Levi. Covering her ears with a pillow to block out Levi's snores, Yasmin closed her eyes tight and tried to imagine a different world. One where she was alone. Where nobody would bother her.

And where Levi had never existed.

CHAPTER TWENTY-FOUR
Worse to Worserer

Cracking open one bloodshot eye, Yasmin awoke on Saturday morning with the same headache she'd gone to sleep with. She'd been restless all night, thanks mostly to Levi's snoring.

She raised her head from the pillow. Where was that walking furball anyway? He usually woke Yasmin up with his own rendition of *Morning Has Broken*.

She rolled over in bed to face the laundry basket.

It was standing upright, with her dirty laundry folded neatly inside.

Yasmin shot straight up in bed, wildly looking around the room. He wasn't by the TV, up on the window sill *or* hiding under the bed. Jumping up, she rushed over to her cupboard, threw it open and rummaged through the clothes inside. He wasn't there either.

Had Levi actually . . . gone?

Yasmin rubbed her bleary eyes. And that's when she saw it. A little note placed on top of the folded laundry. With caution, she crept over and picked it up.

Dear Yasmin

By now you've probably realised that I've gone. I've taken all me stuff and tried to tidy up best I could. You might want to wash me towels though.

I know you sent a text to Mama Llama. You can probably guess that that breaks like a million rules for Seen Not Herd. You ain't supposed to know she exists! And it's my fault.

I'm a proud llama, Yasmin. I don't like saying when I messed up but . . . I messed up. I thought I knew what you needed. I thought I could prove Mama Llama wrong, but I guess I'm no good at this guardian llama stuff. She's got a good punishment for me though, don't you worry. I don't deserve to be a magic llama.

I only wanted to help.

I'm sorry, Yasmin. Really. I hope you find your voice one day.

From,
Levi

Levi had gone.

He'd finally gone!

And Yasmin felt . . .

Awful.

A single tear fell from her cheek and landed on Levi's note, soaking through the ink. Levi had wanted to help her stand up for herself, and she finally had – by dobbing him in to his boss! Now he was facing the ultimate punishment.

She put her head in her hands. What had she done?

I only wanted to help.

Yasmin knew what it was like to want to help people. That was why she'd volunteered to go to OLD in the first place. And she certainly knew what it felt like to try, and fail.

Now Levi was gone.

Yasmin was so wrapped up in the shock of Levi (Leave-i?) leaving that she didn't hear the stomps heading upstairs. Ammi flung open the door with the strength of a sumo wrestler.

'YASMINSHAH,' she boomed, towering over her daughter. 'THETEACHERHASJUSTTOLDME –'

Uh-oh.

' – THATYOUGOTDETENTION – TWICE?AND . . . YOUWEREKICKEDOUTOFOLD?' Ammi looked like she might start shooting lasers out of her eyes.

Papa materialised behind her, his eyebrows sloping into an angry frown. 'No daughter of mine

will be seen getting detentions and throwing tantrums IN PUBLIC!' he boomed, wagging his finger so hard that it looked like it was going to fall off. 'I have already rung Daadi, you will be staying with her for the summer. But not only that. I'm afraid you've gone too far this time . . . !'

Yasmin groaned to herself. She had already been kicked out of OLD. What more could they take away from her?

Papa's finger stopped wagging. He held it straight in the air, his face deadly serious as he came closer to Yasmin. 'You are *forbidden* from playing checkers . . . EVER. AGAIN.'

CHAPTER TWENTY-FIVE
Listen to Me!

Yasmin was running, her rucksack bumping on her back. On and on and on she ran. Down Brick Lane, past the curry houses and the sweet shops. Still in her spotty pyjamas and slippers, might I add. She dodged through the crowds, moving her legs as fast as she could and crying bitterly. In her mind, she saw Papa's face, so disappointed and angry. And even worse, those formidable words, *You are* forbidden *from playing checkers.*

She passed the traffic lights at the end of the road. Through her tears, she could see all the people waiting at the bus stop, staring at the girl running down the street in her PJs. Her cheeks were red and her lungs ached. She just wanted to get away. Away from Ammi and Papa and everyone.

When she reached a roundabout, Yasmin slowed down. She didn't know where she was. Everything seemed unfamiliar. In a hurry to get away from the road, she spotted a fence behind some bushes. She could at least duck behind there for a while, until her parents stopped following her.

She took the rucksack off and threw it over the fence into tall green grass. She heard it hit the ground with a hard thud from a short distance away. Then, unsure how to scale the fence unharmed, she followed it around to a patch where the fence panels were loose. She squeezed through the opening and pushed through the shrubbery, pulling the strap of her bag towards her.

As the undergrowth cleared, she could make out a series of little sheds. This definitely wasn't someone's house. Where was she?

She started to weave her way through the long grass, eventually finding herself on a small dirt path. On both sides were the little sheds with wire fences.

Yasmin approached and peered through.

All of a sudden, a flash of feathers came flying at her from inside the fence. It was a chicken!

Yasmin leapt back, startled.

There were more pens running down either side of the dirt path. Walking on, she saw geese, ducks, turkeys and even a pheasant. What was this place – a bird hotel?

Written above one of the sheds was a sign:

CITY FARM

Yasmin had never heard of City Farm. But maybe it was a good place to hide until she could figure out where to go next. There was no way she was ever, ever, *ever* going home.

The farm was surprisingly empty for a Saturday morning, apart for the odd worker mucking out the sheds. Yasmin walked all around, surveying the animals. There was a small muddy sty holding two pongy pigs. A little further down the lane was a larger pen containing a small herd of sheep, huddled together like heavy clouds. On the other side of the lane was a whole clearing for a couple of sad looking cows, simultaneously munching and pooing.

She turned a corner into the last section of the farm. There were two large, grassy paddocks. In the

right paddock were horses, but in the left paddock,
lying still in the fresh green grass . . .

Were three llamas.

One of which had a suspicious brown stain over
its back legs.

Yasmin gasped.

Levi?

The large, living llama Levi's eyes were wide with surprise. He started to run up to the fence.

A voice came from behind Yasmin.

'YASMINSTOPRIGHTTHERE!' Ammi shouted, huffing and puffing.

Papa was not far behind, thoroughly out of breath. 'You are in so much trouble!' he called, leaning against a wall for support.

Levi rushed up to the wooden fence behind Yasmin. 'Yassy, I'm so sorry! Lemme help!'

Yasmin desperately wanted to apologise to Levi – because it was Levi, it absolutely was, even though he was bigger and smellier and more real. And he still had his voice! But she could not be seen talking to a llama in front of her parents.

Levi gently nudged the back of her head with his nose. 'Now's your chance, love! Let 'em have it!'

'You will be going to Pakistan as soon as school finishes,' Papa scolded. 'If your own father cannot improve your behaviour, then only Daadi can help.'

'You ain't scared of that old lady,' Levi countered.

'YOURBEHAVIOURISAWFUL!'

'Now's your chance to be *heard*!' Levi urged.

'What have I done to deserve such an unruly daughter? My *only* daughter!'

'Ignore 'em,' Levi said. 'Just listen to what's inside yer own noggin!'

'NOMORECHECKERSNOMOREFUN!'

'Come on Yasmin,' Levi begged. 'Don't let them talk to you like this!'

'You should follow the example of your older brothers, such good boys!'

'LISTENTOME!' shouted Ammi.

'Listen to me!' shouted Levi.

'Listen to me!' shouted Papa.

'Everybody SHUT IT!!!'

Yasmin gazed around her, alarmed. Where had that extremely low and booming voice come from?

Papa's mouth was wide open in shock. Ammi

clutched her hand to her chest.

'YASMIN,' said Ammi. Slowly, for once.

'DID

'YOU

'JUST

'SPEAK?'

'Ha! I knew your voice would be weird,' Levi
quipped. 'Now I know why your brothers used to
call you Trombone.' Wait. Had that voice just come
from her? Had Yasmin just . . . spoken?

No, not spoken – *yelled*?

Yasmin coughed a little and swallowed. Her hands were screwed up tightly into fists and her head was pounding. Now that she'd started, she couldn't stop.

'YOU listen to ME!' she commanded in her deep voice, quite enjoying the sensation. 'All my life I've put up with you all blabbering on, telling me what to do, when I should do it and how. Well, I've had enough! None of those pranks were me! Not the pepper in my napkin! Not the rubbish! Not the tea trolley at OLD! Not the fish!'

'The fish?' Papa asked.

'Not anything!' said Yasmin. 'I wasn't the one who put hair dye in the washing machine last summer! And the hairdryer didn't break because I was using it as a microphone, it just BROKE! None of it was my fault! But there wasn't any point telling you because you *don't listen*! But, now, I'm finally going to speak up for myself.

'I deserve to be heard!'

She caught herself and took a sudden breath. Spinning around, she looked at Levi's big, real, stupid face. He was grinning a wonky-toothed grin and nodding.

'You do,' he murmured.

'So, Ammi and Papa.' Yasmin spun back around. 'I've decided to live here now, with the sheep. Then, when I'm old enough, I'll join OLD and finally be able to play in the checkers tournament final. So goodbye. I hope you have nice lives.'

Ammi gave a little panicked yelp and sat down on

the floor.

'Yasmin, where has this . . .' Papa searched for the word – 'confidence come from?'

Yasmin shrugged. Then it clicked. Who was the most demanding, assertive, loud and downright annoying person she knew?

Well, not person.

Had Levi actually done it? Had he managed to help her?

Yasmin wiped the tears from her eyes and started towards the sheep pen. As she walked past her parents, she expected one last shout or one last scolding. But Papa was staring silently at the floor. Then, as she passed Ammi (who had stood up again), something strange happened.

Ammi grabbed Yasmin's hand and pulled her in for a big, silent hug.

'I am so sorry, Yasmin,' Ammi said, in a volume normal to a human being. 'We have not been fair to you.'

In terms of the greatest shocks of all time, Yasmin decided this would come in at number one. Ammi was apologising to *her*?

Ammi reached into her bag and brought out her purse, which she slowly unzipped. Spilling out came four years' worth of little scraps of paper and notes.

'I've kept them all,' Ammi explained, picking through the pile. 'This one is my favourite.'

PLEASE PLEASE PLEASE
CAN I GET A
CHECKERS
BOARD
I WANT
TO LEARN
TO PLAY!

She held up a note that said: *Please please please can I get a checkers board? I want to learn to play!* It must have been from a couple of years ago, when Yasmin had first started going to OLD.

'I am so proud of you, Yasmin.' Ammi stroked Yasmin's head. 'And especially how good you have become at checkers. That's why we got you that book of logic puzzles, to help you with your tournament.'

Yasmin suddenly felt a guilty pang rise in her stomach. The birthday present she'd thought was rubbish was actually very, *very* thoughtful. Her parents *had* been listening. Just in their own way.

'My *jaan* . . .' Papa was pulling a very funny face indeed. Yasmin realised with surprise that he was trying not to cry. 'I didn't know you could miss something you've never heard, but how I've missed your voice!' He pulled Yasmin into a big hug and sniffed back a few tears. 'Of course you deserve to be heard. It's hard when you are the youngest of the family. I was the youngest too, and your aunties have always tried to speak over me. Even now that I am the man of the house.'

Yasmin giggled. Ammi was suppressing a smirk too. All that talk of being man of the house had just been Papa trying to stand up to his big sisters.

Papa finally released Yasmin from his airtight hug. 'I'm so glad you have finally told us how you *feel*. Now we know, we will never ignore you again.'

The advice Ezra had given her earlier suddenly popped into Yasmin's head.

'So . . . ' she ventured. 'Now that I've blinked the little light on the dashboard, you know what's wrong with my engine?'

Ammi looked puzzled.

'Telling us what's wrong means that we can help you solve the problem, yes,' said Papa. 'And you have finally blinked the light on the dashboard. Now come here and give us a cuddle!'

Yasmin let herself be squashed in an Ammi and

Papa sandwich.

'So, Yasmin,' Ammi said, getting back to business. 'Your punishment is, of course, cancelled. You will not go to Pakistan to stay with Daadi, and you will play checkers whenever you want.'

'But you've booked the plane tickets,' said Yasmin. Ammi and Papa were not likely to waste money. 'Who will stay with Daadi for the summer now?'

Ammi and Papa thought for a moment.

'Well,' Papa pondered. 'It would be nice for Hamza and Tariq to visit Pakistan.'

'Who?' Yasmin asked.

'Your *brothers*, Yasmin,' Papa said worriedly.

'Ohhhh! Tall Brother and Short Brother,' said Yasmin.

Papa chuckled and ruffled Yasmin's hair.

'What a good idea!' Ammi agreed. 'It would be good for the boys to spend a summer with their Daadi. I'm sure they would love it.'

They released Yasmin from the sandwich hug and

each took one of her hands. As they led her out of the paddocks, Yasmin suddenly had a thought. A thought that didn't concern Ammi or Papa, or Daadi, or even checkers.

She turned her head. Levi had been quiet the whole time she and her parents had been speaking. Now he was standing at the locked gate of the paddock, staring after Yasmin. He was still smiling, but Yasmin could see the sadness in his eyes.

He was trapped as a real llama now. The one thing he hated. And she was the only one who could help him.

CHAPTER TWENTY-SIX
Yasmin to the Rescue!

By the end of the evening, the blackboard behind Yasmin's bed was *chock-a-block*.

Scribbles of calculations, a huge pros and cons

list, a floor plan of the City Farm and a map of Brick Lane filled the space. The blackboard looked like Yasmin's brain had thrown up all over it.

And it was all leading up to her greatest mission yet.

By 9pm, Yasmin had the plan sorted in her head. She just needed a little help. Grabbing her school planner, she turned to the class directory and called Ezra's home number.

After a few rings a woman with a warm voice answered the phone. 'Hello?'

'Hi, sorry to call late,' said Yasmin. 'Please could I speak to Ezra? It's his friend, Yasmin.'

'Oh, hi Yasmin. Ezra is supposed to be in bed, but you can have five minutes.'

There were a few moments in which Yasmin could just hear a shuffling noise and muffled voices before Ezra came to the phone.

'Yasmin?'

'Hi Ezra, it's me.'

'Yasmin, you're speaking! This is great!'

'Yeah. I'm still getting used to it.' Yasmin coughed a little. She'd done a lot of shouting today, and her voice wasn't used to it. 'I'm really sorry about storming off at OLD. I wasn't angry at you.'

'That's okay. My mum explained that I should just "give you space". Whatever that means.'

Yasmin smiled. Ezra's mum sounded nice. 'Could you help me with something? Would you meet me at City Farm tomorrow at eleven?'

Ezra moved the phone away from his mouth. Yasmin heard him yell: 'MUM! CAN I GO TO CITY FARM WITH YASMIN TOMORROW?'

His mum yelled back, 'HAVE YOU DONE ALL YOUR HOMEWORK?'

'YES!!!'

'ALL RIGHT! NOW GET TO BED!'

Ezra came back to the phone. 'She said yes!'

'Great,' Yasmin said happily. 'I'll see you there. Bye.'

'Bye!'

Yasmin clicked the phone back in its holder and settled into bed. She closed her eyes, took a deep breath and said *out loud*:

'Don't worry Levi. I'm on it.'

CHAPTER
TWENTY-SEVEN
The Grand Checkers
Tournament
Final

It was a scorching hot summer's day – the hottest there had been for years, according to the weather presenter on the news. Everyone in Whitechapel was frolicking through sprinklers in their gardens with ice lollies dripping down their hands. Everyone, that is, apart from Yasmin and Ezra. They were trotting down Brick Lane with a real-life llama.

Attendance at OLD had apparently been at an all-time low since Yasmin left. The members were Bored with a capital B. There was no drama, no mayhem and nothing to talk about. So when Ezra called Mr Matthews and explained that he was helping the City Farm rent out a new type of therapy animal, Mr Matthews had been over the moon.

He wasn't aware exactly what type of animal it was yet.

Which brings us to Ezra knocking on the door of OLD and giving Yasmin a big thumbs up. She was hanging back, holding the reins of a llama who wouldn't keep still. It was a big day for OLD, what with the visit from the new therapy animal. And it also happened to be . . .

The Grand Final of the OLD Checkers Tournament!

'Remind me again why this is a good idea,' Levi hissed, fidgeting against the rope.

'Mama Llama will see that you're a changed man,' Yasmin whispered back. 'I mean, llama. Helping the community, doing good deeds . . .'

'Spitting on the elderly . . .'

'Levi!' Yasmin tugged his rope.

'I'm jokin'!' said Levi. 'I won't spit. If this will help turn me back into a toy llama again, I'll do anything you want.'

He kicked his foot against the ground and shook his matted head. Even as a real llama, Levi was still scabby.

The door creaked open. Mr Matthews craned his neck out.

'Ah, Ezra, you're here,' he said. 'And you've brought . . . an alpaca?'

Levi gasped. 'I'M OFFENDED! WE DON'T ALL LOOK THE SAME.'

'Um actually, it's a llama,' Ezra corrected. 'But I also brought . . .' He gestured to Yasmin. '. . . my grandma!'

I probably should have mentioned that Yasmin, at this particular moment in time, wasn't Yasmin.

You see, since Yasmin had been banned from OLD, she had to enter in disguise. With the help of her aunties earlier in the day, she had gone undercover in a pair of big bloomers, a pink blouse and a knitted shawl. For good measure, Auntie Bibi had even drawn some wrinkles on to Yasmin's

forehead with a felt tip pen. She looked like the real
deal.

To begin with, they weren't sure it would work.
But as Yasmin walked through the door with Levi in
tow, Mr Matthews introduced himself.

'Why hello there!' he said. 'And welcome to the
Octogenarians' London Daycentre!'

'Yeeesssss, I am old.' Yasmin said suddenly in her

low voice. She was a bit nervous and not sure how to behave.

'What have I got myself into?' Levi groaned.

Mr Matthews raised his eyebrows. 'How old exactly are you?'

'Eighty!' Yasmin blurted out. 'Eighty . . . two!'

'And what's the llama's name?'

'Um, uh. Buttercup.'

'You've gotta be jokin' me,' said Levi.

Mr Matthews looked at Ezra, then to Levi and then finally back to Yasmin. 'Brilliant!' he said. 'And what shall I call you, Mrs . . .?'

Yasmin seized up. They hadn't thought of a name! What would be a convincing name for an eighty-two-year-old woman?

'Ummm, O – O . . .' Her eyes darted around the room for help. 'It's, um, Mrs . . .' She was really panicking now. 'Mrs . . . McOld . . . laydee – yes, Mrs McOldlaydee!'

Levi snorted. Yasmin shot him a warning glance.

'Very well then, Mrs McOldlaydee, come on through!' said Mr Matthews. 'I'm afraid it's rather busy today. You see, we were supposed to have our checkers tournament final.'

'Oh? What happened?' Yasmin said in an enquiring tone.

Gilly now came pushing through the crowd, ready to play her part in the master plan. Yasmin had texted her and explained the details.

'Unfortunately, one of our finalists was disqualified,' Gilly announced.

'It was stupid and definitely not a good idea,' Ezra remarked.

Yasmin nudged him. 'What my friend – I mean, my *grandson* means is how unfortunate you had to cancel.'

'It is unfortunate.' Mr Matthews seemed quite frazzled. 'We even have the other OLD group from Brixton visiting for the final. It's actually rather embarrassing. I don't know what to do.'

'I say, Mrs McOldlaydee,' Gilly said in her rehearsed lines. 'Weren't you the Bournemouth checkers finalist a few years back?'

'Why, yes. Yes, I was,' Yasmin replied carefully.

Mr Matthews brightened. 'Do you two know each other?'

'Yes, erm, old friends,' said Gilly. 'ANYWAY, isn't it true that you never got to play in the final match, therefore leaving you longing to finish the competition that you had trained your whole life to partake in?' Gilly was really getting into her role. She must have been rehearsing the lines the night before.

'It's true,' Yasmin sighed. 'Now I will *never* live my dream of playing in a competitive checkers final.'

'There, there, Grandma,' Ezra soothed, though not very convincingly. Acting wasn't his strong point. 'I guess you will just have to DIE never knowing what might have been.'

Levi rolled his eyes. 'It's like an episode of *Eastenders* in 'ere.'

Mr Matthews's eyes lit up. 'Hang on! I think I have an idea!'

Yasmin, Ezra and Gilly held their breath.

'Why don't you take the place in our checkers match?' Mr Matthews exclaimed. 'We can say you qualified in a different area, and no one was good enough to play you, so you had to come here!'

'Oh,' Yasmin said. In her head, she was punching the air. 'Are you sure?'

'Certainly!' Mr Matthews beamed, before quietly adding, 'You'd actually be doing me a favour, with all these people here to see a checkers match.'

'Great, so it's decided, let's go get ready,' Gilly babbled, pulling Yasmin away.

'Don't leave me!' Levi whined, trotting after them. 'There's people trying to *pet* me.'

'Good talking to you.' Ezra reached up and patted Mr Matthews on the head before following Yasmin and Gilly in.

Yasmin sat nervously at the checkers board, fiddling with her shawl. There was no backing out now, especially since she had some very special fans in the audience.

Sitting in a line in the very front row were Ammi, Papa, Auntie Bibi and Auntie Gigi. They had all come specially to watch Yasmin (in disguise) compete in the final. Papa had even tried to give Yasmin some last-minute coaching, despite not knowing the rules.

'Good luck Yasmin!' Papa whispered, leaning towards her. 'You can do it!'

Yasmin was relieved to see a grumpy Levi surrounded by a group of old ladies giving him strokes and trying to brush the knots out of his hair. Good. That was one less distraction to worry about. Sitting on the arm of Gilly's armchair, Ezra caught Yasmin's eye and gave her a big smile. He had been practising with her almost every day to prepare for this.

Everyone was here to support her. Now she just had to win. Not only had she worked her bum off all year, but she wanted that £100 prize.

The small crowd at Yasmin's previous checkers matches had tripled for the final. Every member of OLD, plus the Brixton members, had turned up to see who would win the £100 prize and the coveted Golden Checker Piece. The crowd had come to see a thrilling match, and a thrilling match they would get. Yasmin had won all her matches so far. Why shouldn't she win this one?

But then, in what could rank at number two in the greatest shocks of all time, the crowd parted and her opponent was revealed to be . . .

Mr Matthews.

'Don't think I'll go easy on you just because you're new,' Mr Matthews said as he pulled up his chair.

'Don't think I'll go easy on you just because you're old,' replied Yasmin. 'Like me!' she added quickly, 'because I'm old too.'

Mr Matthews raised an eyebrow. 'Let's just get on with it,' he said.

The judge raised her stopwatch. All the crowd counted down together.

'Three . . . two . . . one . . . go!'

Mr Matthews made the first move, hopping his

black checker piece forward. *POW!*

Yasmin moved her left piece forward. *WHOOSH!*

Mr Matthews responded, mirroring her move. *KAPOW!*

Stealthily, Yasmin hopped her white piece over his, capturing it. *SLAM!* The crowd cheered.

'Kick his butt!' Levi yelled, dodging a woman trying to put a bow around his neck.

But Mr Matthews had planned this. Just as quickly, he hopped his piece over Yasmin's, capturing it for himself. *WHAM!* The crowd gasped.

On and on this went, back and forth, with the crowd going, 'Ooooooooooooooohhhhhhhhhhh!' and 'Aaaaaaaaaahhhhhhhhhhhhhhhhhhhh!' until both Yasmin and Mr Matthews only had half their pieces left on the board.

They were at a tie.

But Yasmin had a plan. She had devised a strategy that would distract Mr Matthews long enough for her to make the winning move. If she could just keep her nerve . . .

She made her best (pretend) worried face – scrunching up her nose and squinting her eyes – and moved a piece forward slowly.

'Yasmin!' Gilly called out in alarm. 'Are you sure?'

'Please refrain from advising the competitors!' the judge barked.

Mr Matthews smiled to himself and moved his

piece closer. Much, *much* closer to Yasmin's king piece. The piece that would win *him* the game.

Just as Yasmin had known he would.

Mr Matthews thought that he was going to be able to capture Yasmin's king.

'Mr Matthews,' Yasmin said seriously, looking the group leader in the eye.

'Yes?'

She moved her piece forward. 'I believe I have just won the game.'

Mr Matthew's eyes widened in horror. By moving to attack Yasmin's king, he had left his own king exposed!

'Nooooooo!' he yelled, holding his hands to his head.

'Don't be a sore loser!' Gilly scolded, patting him roughly on the back.

'Mrs McOldlaydee! Mrs McOldlaydee!' the crowd cheered. It was a bit of a tongue twister. They lifted Yasmin's chair in celebration – and then quickly thought better of it when many of their backs cracked loudly. Ammi, Papa and the aunties were cheering so loudly that Yasmin noticed a few OLD members readjusting their hearing aids.

'THAT'SMYDAUGHTER!' Ammi screamed, leaving many OLD members commenting that she looked very good for her age.

Gilly kissed Yasmin on the forehead. 'You did it, my girl! I'm so happy, I could cry!'

'Me too!' Ezra added enthusiastically. 'Well, maybe not cry. But I knew you could do it Yas— I mean, Grandma.' He winked.

'I always knew you were a winner, Yassy!' Levi called over from the side of the room, where a lady was giving him a head massage 'You know . . . these oldies aren't so bad after all . . .'

Yasmin pulled Gilly and Ezra into a hug, smiling from ear to ear. All her hard work had paid off. Practice really did make perfect.

It was unfortunately down to Mr Matthews to

present the Golden Checker Piece to Yasmin. They made a small stage out of some upturned fruit and veg boxes for Yasmin to stand on, which she did, proudly holding her £100 prize cheque. Ammi took about a million pictures and Papa even posted it in the family text chat with the caption: *My daughter the champion! She learned everything she knows from me.*

As Mr Matthews brought out the glittering trophy, the audience applauded. It was the shiniest thing Yasmin had ever seen, shaped like a large checker piece and mounted on a wooden stand.

'For outstanding game play and tactical strategy,' Mr Matthews announced, 'I would like to award this trophy to ... *Yasmin Shah.*'

Yasmin's eyes bugged at Mr Matthews.

'How did you know?' she gasped.

Mr Matthews chuckled. ' I knew as soon as we started the match. There's only one person I know who can play that well. You might not be an official member of OLD, but you really do deserve this, Yasmin.'

He stretched out his hand to shake, but Yasmin threw her arms around his neck in a hug instead, making Mr Matthews blush.

Ezra got out his phone and shouted, 'Come on, give her the trophy!'

Mr Matthews quickly handed the trophy over to Yasmin, and she smiled like an Olympic athlete with the gold medal. She had dreamt of this moment so many times – and now that it was happening, it was even better. In her dreams, she'd never expected to have a best friend standing there cheering for her. But there Ezra was, clapping longer than anyone else and chanting her name. Yasmin knew that she would remember this moment forever.

After the award ceremony Gilly took Yasmin aside. 'What are you going to do now, Yasmin? You can't stop playing checkers just because you're banned from OLD.'

'Don't worry. I've started a checkers club at school with Ezra,' Yasmin told her. 'So people who prefer a bit of quiet have somewhere to go at lunchtime.'

'Oh, that's wonderful!' Gilly said. 'But you will come back and see me, won't you? I always have more fun with you than I do with this ancient lot.'

Yasmin nodded. 'Of course, Gilly! We can go and feed naan to the mice in the park and make the ducks jealous.'

Gilly giggled. 'That sounds like my kind of game. What will you do with your prize money?'

Yasmin looked at her family getting tea and biscuits and chattering as loudly as ever.

'I have a good idea,' she said.

CHAPTER TWENTY-EIGHT
Your Local Community Llama

Yasmin sprang out of bed on the first day of Year Six. Downstairs, she could already hear a massive commotion as her family clanged about, preparing breakfast. Pots and pans collided as the family raised their voices over the hubbub. Even with her two brothers away in Pakistan, the house wasn't any quieter. (Un)luckily for Tall Brother and Short Brother, their flight had been delayed, so they were spending an extra week with Daadi.

Yasmin looked at the postcard pinned up on her wall that she had received from them last week. Yasmin chuckled. She had a feeling her brothers wouldn't be teasing her quite so much in the future.

Dear Ammi, Papa, Auntie Bibi, Auntie Gigi . . . and Yasmin,
We are having a wonderful time with Daadi in Pakistan. We have definitely
become better people for — oh good, she's gone. Help us! It's so boring
here! We want to come home! We promise we will be good and never tease
Yasmin again. We're sorry! If Daadi comes back and reads this over our
shoulders she will make us wash individual grains of rice again. HELP!

Hamza and Tariq

She called downstairs. 'AMMI!' But she had no chance of being heard over the racket. Walking over to her desk drawer, she pulled out her brand new, top of the range hundred-pound megaphone and aimed it down the stairs.

The megaphone boomed through the house. *'Ammi, can I walk myself to school?'*

'YESYASMINBUTSTICKTOTHEMAINROAD!'

Her family certainly had no problems hearing

her now.

Yasmin got dressed and rushed down the stairs.

'Tell your friend Ezra to come to tea again,' Auntie Bibi said with a smile. 'We've bought an extra chair so no one has to use the wonky stool this time.'

Yasmin nodded, grabbed some breakfast and bounded over to the door in her brand-new school uniform. The jumper was still a bit itchy and the skirt way too long, but she knew this year was going to be completely different.

Checking her watch, she upped her pace and strode along Brick Lane.

She just had one more stop to make before school.

Yasmin found the hole in the fence and crawled through, clearing the weeds away as she made her way into the paddocks of City Farm. She could have used the main entrance, but the secret entrance was always more fun.

As she approached the paddocks at the end of the path, the llamas were being led out for their morning feed. The two white llamas, Daisy and Marigold, clip-clopped sweetly into the paddock and began munching on some grass with contented expressions. A few moments later, and with some resistance, a farm hand emerged from the shed leading a dirty grey llama with a brown stain all over his back legs.

'Levi!' Yasmin ran up to the gates.

The farm hand left Levi by the food trough and went to muck out the shed. When he wasn't looking, Yasmin slipped a packet of chocolate digestives from her bag.

'Ahhhh, that's my girl!' Levi grinned, munching up three biscuits in one go.

'How's it going?' Yasmin asked, wiping the Levi spit from her hand and getting out more biscuits.

'Oh, you know. Same-same,' Levi moaned through

munches. 'Mama Llama said she's impressed with me charity work, but she still needs to see more evidence before she'll turn me back into a toy. I'll have to wait for the beginning of the next moon month and all that malarkey anyway.'

Yasmin chewed her lip.

'What's up? You look like you're constipated,' Levi said with a snort.

Yasmin bopped him on the nose. 'I'm nervous about starting Year Six,' she said. 'It's going to be the first time the other kids have heard me speak since –'

'Since the Purple/Poo Incident!' Levi laughed out loud. 'Don't worry about it, Yassy. Just think about me. I don't care what no one thinks of me, and I'm happy as Larry.' He grinned. There was a huge piece of green grass stuck in his front teeth.

'That's very clear.' Yasmin picked the grass out. 'What if they make fun of me again?'

Levi trotted around in a little circle, thinking.

'You hold yer head high and say in that booming voice of yours, "I'm Yasmin Shah and I deserve to be heard!"' he said. 'Then you can do a little fart as you walk away, leave them to deal with that.'

Yasmin laughed and shook her head. Levi's advice was either complete rubbish or solid gold. She hadn't decided which yet.

'Now get going or you're gonna be late,' Levi said. 'And you're usually a goody two-shoes!'

He was right. School started in fifteen minutes! Leaving the rest of the chocolate digestives in a grassy patch, Yasmin gave Levi one last pat and headed for the secret entrance.

Just before crawling through the little hole, she took one last look back. Levi was munching away, sitting in the grass, a full life-sized real llama. Anyone visiting would think he was just another one of the farm animals.

But then he caught Yasmin's eye, stuck his tongue out and blew a huge raspberry.

Yasmin giggled and headed for school.

You can take the llama out of the toy.

But you can't take Levi out of the llama.

That's not the last you've heard of Yasmin and Levi!

Join them for another hilarious adventure packed with LOLs, llamas, dramas and, this time, secret agents! (Shhh!)